STOP SPITTING AT YOUR BROTHER!

LIFE LESSONS OF A ROCKY MOUNTAIN LLAMA

Written and Illustrated by
Diane White-Crane

As told to her by Dudley The-Llama

Aspentree Press
Steamboat Springs, Colorado

Library of Congress Catalog
Card Number 96-85123

ISBN 0-9631322-1-0

First Printing: July 1996

DEDICATION

To my family with love.

*And for Judy Seaver (1945-1996),
my friend who taught me lessons
in courage and caring.*

ACKNOWLEDGEMENTS

Special thanks to my friends, Mary Ann and John Duffey, owners of the Rainbow Park Llama Ranch in Clark, Colorado. Much of the material in this book is based on the real-life experiences of John and Mary Ann's delightful cast of llama characters. To know them is to love them!

Many thanks to my other friends, Ellie Cameron for the desktop composing; to my readers, Tom Bethel, Nan Nelson, Jane Winer, Helen Bayliss, and Anona Fowler; and for Lourana Thomas, John Winkler and Joe Williams for helping to prepare the music.

CONTENTS

CHAPTERS:

PROLOGUE

PATOOIE! SPLAT!

Are you familiar with llamas and the above noise which they sometimes enjoy making?

Just a few short years ago, about all I seemed to know of these somewhat strange-looking creatures is that they like to spit at each other, they hum a lot, and they're good at carrying things for people. That was about it. Then I met Dudley and Sammy, two loveable Rocky Mountain llamas, and they soon taught me everything I probably ever need to know about these delightful animals. After I had spent just a few days with them, Dudley and Sammy had turned me into a dyed-in-the-llama-wool fan.

Before my first experiences with these two characters, though, if you had told me that I would one day write a story not only *about* llamas but also *FOR* a llama, I never would have believed you. But here I am, writing down a collection of llama stories as told to me *by* a llama. So remember--never say never!

"As told to her by a llama?" Right about now, I'll bet you're thinking, "What's she talking about? Llamas are animals, and everyone knows that animals can't talk to humans. This lady must have bats in her belfry!"

Before you reach that conclusion, though, the one about me having bats in my belfry, I hope you'll wait until Chapter III where Dudley will tell you in detail just how he taught me his llama language and helped me to bridge the communication barrier between animals and humans.

At this point, though, I'd like to warn you a little bit about Dudley's personality. For you see, like many young male llamas, Dudley is a very independent and strong-willed fellow, which means that he likes to be his *own* boss and to do things his *own* way. He also likes to have fun while he's at it, but it's sometimes at the expense of others. Unfortunately, these are the kinds of traits which seem to get many a young llama into trouble with the humans who own them. And so it is with our Dudley!

Often impatient with those around him, be they humans or other animals, he frequently misinterprets and complains about their actions. Dudley teases, spits at, and plays tricks on his brother, Sammy, and nobody would ever accuse him of being too humble a soul.

"A llama with an attitude and a mind of his own," is yet another way one of our mutual friends best describes our llama friend. He's usually certain of his opinions, very sure of himself, and sometimes also quite *full* of himself--there's no denying that!

But this animal has another side to him, too, a more tender and loving side, and I think it's important that you know this about him so that you'll give him the benefit of the doubt when he brags about some of the mischievous things he does to others.

Dudley.

Oh, you Gotta' Llove a Llama!

If you scratch his thick wooly surface, I think you'll soon discover that underneath all of his wise guy bragging and teasing, his practical jokes, his lack of patience with others, and his tough-guy llama talk, Dudley is actually a llama with a great big heart.

When all is said and done, it's obvious to us, his family and friends, that this funny character cares about us dearly. Even Dudley's brother, Sammy, the butt of so many of his jokes, takes Dudley's attitudes and words with a grain of salt. For like me, Sammy has learned from experience that whenever we need his help, his friendship or his protection, Dudley will be right there, loyally by our side, willing to protect us-- even with his own life! If he were a dog instead of a llama, I would tell you that Dudley's bark is actually much worse than his bite.

When reading about this llama's exploits, you'll probably notice that Dudley often enjoys playing with human words and using people expressions, even when he gets them all mixed up or doesn't quite understand their exact meanings.

His narrations often go off on tangents, and once he starts to tell you a story, you'll never know for certain which station his train of thoughts will take you to next. So, when you're on a Dudley thought journey, it's best to just fasten your seat belt and ride along with him, enjoying the scenery as you go. His story-telling somehow always manages to bring our train back to the right track. And here's one final Dudley observation. I think that this llama often has to learn his life lessons the *hard* way, and I get the feeling that he wants to save us from having to do that ourselves.

In an effort to make certain that his anecdotes get written down just as he really experiences them, I try never to correct Dudley's mistakes or misconceptions. And that's not always an easy thing for a writer to do!

I hope you'll enjoy looking at life as it's viewed through the eyes of this playful, impish fellow. My wish is that each and every one of you will someday have an opportunity to get to know a real llama first hand, if you don't already.

Spend some time with a live llama, and I think you'll end up agreeing with the words of my song at the back of this book, which is entitled, ***You Gotta' Llove a Llama!***

Diane White-Crane

Dudley & Diane ~ Gold Creek Lake Trail

CHAPTER 1

MY STORY BEGINS -- FROM BIRTH TO SAMMY --

Hi. My name is Dudley, and I'm a *llarge, llikeable, llug of a llama.* Now as far as I know, I've always been a llama, although I often wonder if I might also have been a wild mongoose in some other

life. I say this because my very wise dog friend, Annie, tells me, "You sure act like a big silly goose, Dudley!" And since I don't think that I have ever had feathers or been able to honk, in this life or in any other, I figure that I was more likely a mongoose with fur, rather than a regular old honking goose with feathers. But in this life, at least, I think that I'm

1

just a regular old two-L'd llama.

About six years ago, I entered the world at the Rainbow Mountain Llama Ranch, in Clark, Colorado, born to a very pretty female llama by the name of Morningstar. She's brown and has white marking on her forehead and neck, just like me. She also has beautiful, big, brown doe eyes with long, curly eyelashes which look really sweet on her, but luckily, I've got *guy* eyelashes. One of my boy cousins has curly eyelashes, though, and all the girl llamas think he's "adorable looking." Boy, you could fool me!

I've never met my father, Mr. Spitzer, because he lives on another ranch, but they say he's quite handsome. From time to time I've caught a glimpse of myself in car and truck windows, and I have to tell you that this tree didn't fall far from the old apple!

One time a horse in the neighboring pasture stuck his tongue out at me and called me

Tit for tat...

"Smelly Old Banana Ears," but that was probably just because he was jealous of my good looks. I should have spat at him but Jan, the neighbor lady, was on his back, and I was afraid I'd hit her too and get myself into *BIG* trouble. So instead, I raised up on my tip toes to make myself look taller, and I stuck my tongue out back at him and called him "Smelly old bit-in-the-mouth!" But, the first time he comes near our fence without a rider on him, *PATOOIE!* Right smack dab on his old jealous snout!

Now, in case you're wondering about Clark, Colorado, where I live, it's just a little town about twenty miles north of the Steamboat Ski Area. Do you, or does anyone you know, live in or ever come to visit Steamboat? Lots of people come here to ski in the winter because it's supposedly great fun, although nobody has ever let me try it myself. *LOOK OUT BELOW!* if they ever do!

If you're a lucky person who lives in Steamboat Springs, you already know that the summers here are even prettier and more fun than the winters, especially if you enjoy hiking like I do.

People say that if you ever drive through Clark, don't blink or you'll miss our whole town. There's only one store in town, and it's also the post office, the library, the gas station, bookstore, food store, movie rental place, deli, wine store, and ice cream cone store, all in one. Pretty neat place, huh?

Oh, and for the record, rocky trail ice cream is my favorite Clark Store cone flavor, just in case you ever come out to visit me and want to bring me a little something.

Now like most llamas, my mama gave birth to me while she was standing up. We babies are born standing up, too. At birth, we sort of dive out, landing on our front legs. It's a sight to see!

"GERONIMO!" *KERPLOP!*

At my birth I landed right on my two front feet, all twenty-six pounds of me soaking wet. Since llama babies usually weigh between eighteen and thirty-five pounds, I was just about average in weight. Of course I'm never one to brag, but like most "crias," the name for newborn llamas, I could walk thirty minutes after my birth. People babies usually take about a year to do that, so you can see that we llamas are much stronger and more coordinated than humans.

My mama told me that I was a bit over three and a half feet tall, "mostly all long, wobbly legs!" she laughed. She also told me that when I finally got up and took my first steps, I was still wet and cold. So I toddled unsteadily over to her,

Morningstar with Baby Dudley

snuggled up against her big woolly belly and started to drink some of her warm milk. I always liked her to tell me that story when I was little.

Most llama babies drink only their mother's milk for about half a year. After that we start to eat grasses and hay and oats like the adult llamas, and in my case, figgy newtons and ice cream cones when I can get them. An adult llama usually eats the equivalent of a bale of hay per week, but I'd rather have a bale of figgy newtons if they gave *me* a choice!

When we're first born, baby llamas are very fuzzy and adorable looking and people want to hug our long necks. Our mama llamas try to discourage this because the mamas think all the people attention will make us think of humans as just other llamas, and then we won't learn how to be obedient pack animals willing to take orders from humans. Also, we might be more likely to spit at people if we think of them as just other llamas, especially if the humans tease or annoy us.

As I'm sure you already know, spitting at each other is not considered acceptable behavior among humans, and doing so will almost always get you into *big* trouble. Among llamas, however, spitting is a way of life. It's just our way of telling another llama to "Bug off, buster!"

In herds, spitting is also one of the ways we establish the pecking order in the pasture or on a hiking trail. It's usually lots of fun when you're the spitt*or*, but not so much fun when you're the spitt*ee* on the other end of it!

The word *pack*, as used above, just means *to carry*, and that's what we boy llamas are mainly supposed to do, carry things for people. Humans have been using us as pack animals for about 6,000 years in a cold, steep, mountainous country in South America called Peru.

The first llamas in the United States were brought here about a hundred years ago by some very smart rich people who discovered that we make great live self-fueling mowers for the large lawns on their estates. But word of our many talents and desirable traits as family pets slowly spread, until today, according to one source, there are about 80,000 of us living in North

America.

Luckily, my brother Sammy and I live in the best llama environment--the high Rocky Mountains of Colorado, where the altitude and dry, cool weather are just about perfect conditions for llamas. People now raise llamas in just about every part of the United States, and most llamas probably think that *they* live in the best llama place, but that's a matter of personal taste, I guess.

For instance, I surely don't see how llamas can live in hot and humid places because we have such thick, warm coats of llama wool. And some llamas in warmer climates probably wonder how Sammy and I can stand living in a place which was blanketed with a record-breaking twenty feet of snow in just one month this past January! But as the humans always say, "To each his own."

Many people use our soft, oil-free, lightweight wool to knit or weave toasty-warm blankets, hats and sweaters, and it almost never shrinks. The mom in my family says, "Weavers pay up to ten dollars an ounce for llama wool," but I don't have the slightest idea what dollars or ounces are. All I know is that where we live, Sammy and I need our heavy coats to protect us from the cold winters. So I'm surely grateful that our owners don't sheer us like sheep. Brrrrrr. It makes me cold just to think about that!

By the way, if you like to knit with llama

wool, I wouldn't mind receiving a llama sweater some Christmas, size 2xL-medium, purple/red. Or maybe you could just order me one from the L. L. Llamabean catalog?

By the time I was almost two years old, my mama llama had given birth to two other babies after me, Lucky and Lucy. Now Lucky and Lucy sure sound like better llama names to me than Dudley, and I can't imagine how I got *Dudley* for my name, but Dudley it is, and Dudley I am, and that's just the way the cookie bounces!

If they'd left it up to me, I personally would have chosen a name like *LLawrence Llama II* because it sounds so important. Or maybe even *L.L. Llamabean,* so I could get lots of packages from the mailman. But nobody asked me. Whatever you want to call me, though, is O.K., as long as you never call me *Llate-For-Llunch*!

Like my mama, most female llamas have a new baby every year from age one-and-a-half until they become old grandmamas, if you can imagine that! We llamas usually live for about twenty years, so females can bring a lot of babies into the world in their lifetime. And because they can make these baby llamas, females cost a lot more than males do, just in case you ever want to buy one for somebody for a birthday present.

Llamas do make very nice presents, but you probably shouldn't ever gift wrap one or tie a big bow on him or her. If you do, the present will probably just *EAT* its own gift wrapping, if you

know what I mean!

Unfortunately, because they're usually kept busy making all these babies, the female llamas rarely get to go anywhere. Generally speaking, the boy llamas are used as the pack animals and get to go on trips while the girl llamas have to stay home all the time with their busy babies in the pre-school pasture.

Somehow I don't think this is very fair. Raising babies is hard work, especially if the babies act like *me* when I was little!

My first year and a half were spent chasing and romping with all of the other llama youngsters in one of these pre-school pastures where the babies and mama llamas are all kept

Mamas with their babies

together. We babies certainly were given a lot of nursing and motherly attention, so it was pretty hard to get away with much mischief. Somebody's mama was always watching over you, even if your own mama was busy eating grass or caring for her latest baby.

Now, the baby girls pretty much minded,

Mischievous Babies

but we boys were a different story, and guess who was their ringleader? Righto! So unfortunately for me, I was always getting into trouble with one mama llama or another.

"Dudley, stop your spitting! That's terribly impolite!" "Dudley, stop nipping at your sister!!" "Young man, you put that grain bucket down before the people see what you're trying to do to it!" And "blah, blah, blah," as you can just imagine!

So, after a year and a half of this, my owners

felt I was ready to *fly the coop*, feathers and wings or no feathers and wings!

My mama came to me and said, "Dudley, sweetheart, the ranch people have decided to send you to live with a very nice family, and I also think that you're ready to do that now. You're very independent and able to make it on your own now in the world."

"WOW!" I thought. "Go out into the world on my very own?"

Something about that idea sounded very scary to me, but something else about it sounded most inviting. I knew that there had to be fun adventures out in the big world beyond our pre-school pasture, without all of the overly-protective mama llama supervision, and I was certainly ready, willing, and able to give it a try.

The following week five very strange strangers came to the ranch in a big blue truck which pulled a trailer behind it. There were two big humans, three smaller humans of various sizes, and a big black girl dog. They walked over to our pasture and began talking about me and about llamas in general, "Blah, blah, blah, blah." Pointing right at me, one of the girl kids said, "Isn't he cute, dad? Can we have him?"

"Have who?," I hummed. "And yes, I *AM cute*. Glad you noticed, kid! Want to see me jump?" I did one of my cute stiff-legged llama bounces for them and they all laughed.

Then the big man pointed at me and said to the girl dog, "Well, what do you think about that spunky guy, Annie girl? Should we take him home for Sammy?" The girl dog wagged her tail and barked loudly, "Ja, ja. Home for Sammy!"

"Amazing," I thought! "A talking dog! Whatever will they think of next? And just *who* or *what* is a sammy?"

Suddenly, before I even realized what was happening, one of the ranch people put a rope around my neck and said, "Come on Dudley, it's time to say goodby to your mama and then go to your new home."

"Oh dear!" I thought, "Say goodby to my mama?"

He took me over to Morningstar, and she said, "Son, my little love, there's no denying you've been a bit of a handful, but I've enjoyed every minute of you! You're a very funny, special guy, and I'll never forget you. I'll always love and be proud of you, sweetheart."

"Oh no." I thought, as my heart sank down into to my feet. I barely managed to say a quick "I love you, too, mama," and they were leading me off, away from her. She blew a goodby kiss to me, and I did the same back to her. Later, I wished that I had remembered to thank her for all of her patience and loving care, and that I had told her that I would never forget her, either. But it had all happened too fast for me to do that and

no more words would come out of my dry mouth-
-a real *first for me!*

"*This must all be part of a bad dream,*" I thought, but I couldn't seem to wake up and have it end. My stomach hurt, my heart ached, and suddenly I didn't want to go out into the world on my own anymore. I wanted to stay right there with my mama! *But nobody was giving me that choice.*

As they led me to the blue truck, she called out, "Now you be a good llama, sweetie, and please mind your new family."

"Mind your new family? Mama, did you just say 'Mind your new family'?" I replied in a weak, little voice.

"Yes, son. Remember to do that."

"Oh," I said, disappointed and worried.

I sure didn't like the sound of that last bit of advice, but for the time being I cooperated and climbed into the trailer like they wanted. "What would be my fate?" I wondered.

13

Then I started to cry, *GREAT BIG* llama tears.

It's perfectly O.K. for boy llamas to cry sometimes, I know now, but back then I was sure glad I was inside of the trailer where none of the other boy llamas could see my tears.

* * * * * *

I rode in the trailer for just a short time before we stopped--about ten minutes--and I thought, "So much for going out into the big world!" My curiosity stopped my crying, thank goodness, and they opened the trailer door and led me out to a pretty pasture filled with lots of delicious hay and other good grasses. That was the first thing I noticed.

Much to my surprise, the *second* thing I noticed was a white woolly boy llama, about my age, already in the pasture, grazing away. He looked up and seemed truly excited and delighted to see me! You see, we llamas are herd animals and very social beings, and so we need to be around at least one other llama to be happy. Until I arrived, he had been all alone out there, poor guy.

This other boy llama hurried over to me, very cautiously took a little sniff of my wool, and then he hummed non-stop, "Hi! Welcome! I'm Sammy. Who are you? They told me they were going to bring you. I'm sure glad you're here. I've started to get very lonesome for a

14

companion. What's your name? Where have you come from? You smell *GREAT!* Just like a whole llama ranch! Do you like to play? Want some oats? Want to see the inside of our barn now? How old are you? What's the *matter* with you, can't you hum?"

Well, I didn't hum anything back to him because, you see, I like to take a few minutes to get to know somebody before I'm friendly with them. That's called being *aloof* or *standoffish,* and I learned it by watching the barn cats back at my ranch. Barn cats are great at being aloof, and that's a trait I greatly admire and try to copy whenever possible.

The dad told me this Sammy and I were to become adopted brothers. I wasn't sure what "adopted" meant, but I figured that I'd be able to handle it.

And so, that's how Sammy and I first met.

All in all, living together has been a good arrangement. We get along pretty well most of the time, although, like brothers and sisters everywhere, we *do* have our differences.

Actually, Sammy almost never has differences with me because he's a well-behaved, *perfect* llama. I, on the other hand, am *not.* I have a lot of self-respect, and I like to do things for people only if I think the things will be fun and interesting. Fortunately, I think most things are. But Sammy is another story. He willingly does whatever he's ordered to do, no questions asked, and the people think he's "such an angel" because of this. Then they give this "angel llama" lots of praise and attention

and, frankly, it makes me very jealous!

Being such a *perfect* llama, Sammy also likes to be fussed over, hugged and cuddled by the people, while I don't. I like to take care of myself, if you please, and I don't think that boy llamas should like that gushy stuff, but Sammy disagrees. So, everybody makes such a big fuss over how wonderful *Mr. Perfect* is. That makes me pretty mad sometimes, and so *PATOOIE!* I spit at Sammy and bite his ears. The people get very angry at me when I do this because Sammy, of course, just ignores what I do to him and won't spit or bite back.

Let's face it. Sammy is definitely a Mr. *Goody-Two-Shoes,* and they aren't always easy to live with. But to be honestly perfect with you, Goody-Two-Shoes or not, I'm still glad that Sammy's my brother. Don't tell anybody, especially Sammy, but down deep I really respect him. I wish that I could be a better-behaved llama myself but it just isn't in my nature. I'm just not that kind of guy. I'm more like that kind of guy's opposite.

If Sammy had his way, though, I'd bet you that he would just as soon prefer us to live in the big house with the humans, the dog and the cats.

According to my expert source, Annie Dog, some llamas actually do live as indoor house pets with people. They even lie on the floor with their legs tucked under them and watch the T.V. machines. Some llamas are taught to ride in station wagons and vans in that position, too.

As for me, the only building I've even spent any real time in is our barn during snowstorms, and I'm proud to say that I only travel standing upright in a trailer, the way God meant for llamas to travel! However, I *do* tuck my legs under me at

night when I'm sleeping or resting in the pasture, but never when I travel.

We llamas are taught to lie down or "Kush!" on command. I make them say it to me about three or four times before I lie down, but Sammy, of course, kushes on the first "Kush!" It's disgusting.

Now, supposedly these indoor sissy llamas also have big litter boxes inside of the people houses, if you can imagine that, just like huge cats I guess! I'll bet you a *llarge llicorice* that *llama llavatory llatrines llikely* use up *llarge lloads* of *lloosly-llayered llama llitter.*

How's *that* for a good *llama-l-litter-ation*? Heh, heh.

In case you're wondering how Annie Dog happens to know so much about indoor and outdoor llamas, she learns about things from shows she watches on the T.V. machine. Annie tells me, "The nature program and *Mr. Ed* reruns are my favorite programs, but Claire loves the Sesame Seed show the best and it's very educational." It's hard to imagine how a show about a sesame seed could be that interesting, but Annie says it is.

Anyway, she watches this machine a lot with little Claire. The family thinks she's just a big dog snoozing by the T.V. machine, little realizing that she's listening to and digesting the knowledge. Annie Dog says that she learns all about things in the big world this way. Then she passes this good information on to Yours Truly, and that, my friends, is the main reason why I'm such a smart llama, especially when it comes to the topic of llamas!

For instance, according to Annie, some people use llamas as jogging companions. Other llamas are used for carrying clubs for people

Indoor Llama
Nose-Nuzzlers!

when they go hunting for little white, bouncy round golf birds that sail through the air after people hit them with a skinny club.

Some fancy-pants, long-haired llamas are raised just to do nothing but show off in llama shows and others just have to father babies.

Many sheep ranchers use llamas to guard their livestock. We llamas are very protective, and we scare away predators like coyotes, bears, and mountain lions from sheep flocks at night with our shrill alarms and angry, aggressive behavior. Llamas even lead sheep to shelter during storms, since sheep aren't smart enough to do that on their own. That's probably why Annie dog calls sheep "air heads."

Oh, and before I forget, one more thing about indoor versus outdoor llamas...the way I look at it is this. If God had meant for us llamas to live inside of people houses, He wouldn't have given us such thick, warm woolen coats to wear. We'd have to wear clothes, just like people.

Sarah, one of our kids, has a cute toy llama which is dressed in pajamas, but let me tell you right now that we Rocky Mountain llamas *NEVER EVER* wear pajamas!

I wouldn't mind it, however, if they put a T.V. machine in the barn for us to watch during long snowstorms when we're stuck inside for hours and hours. Sometimes the snow gets so deep, we can't even see out the windows. It gets pretty boring in there with nothing to do but eat old, dried out hay and tease Sammy, although I wouldn't ever want to completely give *that* up!

When I was new to my family, I used to hide things in the barn when I got bored, like buckets and brushes and tools and lead ropes,

and it would drive the dad absolutely nuts! He'd always blame the children. And, HA! I loved it!

But one time Christopher, our boy kid, and Sarah, his sister, set a trap for me and they took a photo of me hiding a bucket.

Well, the jig was up, my goose was cooked and the proof was in the pudding. They'd caught me red-hooved with my two toes in the cookie jar!

So, the dad gave me "a good talking to," as he likes to call it, and now I don't dare hide anything on him anymore. But even when the humans misplace something, guess who the first suspect is? Right! Me! Pretty unfair, huh? But as the dad always tells Christopher, "That's what happens when you establish a reputation."

Now that I've told you a little about myself and my brother, Sammy, I'd like to tell you what the rest of my family is like. The information about my family which I am about to give you in the next chapter is the absolute truth, the whole truth, and nothing but the truth, or my name isn't Dusty. *Oops*! I mean, *Dudley!*

CHAPTER 2

ANNIE DOG, THE CATS

AND MY PEOPLE

annie Dog

If you ask me, they're quite a strange bunch, all of the living creatures inside of the big house on the other side of the irrigation ditch!

My house family consists of two large humans and three smaller ones of various sizes, a big bossy dog and two nosy cats. Now, I can't imagine for the life of me how such a mixed menagerie can all stand living together in the same building, but I guess they do. I hope they all at least have separate stalls!

Luckily for us, Sammy and I only have to put up with each other in our barn, if you don't count the field mice and insects which manage to escape cat capture.

Among all the living beings in that big house, my most favorite is the dog, so I'll tell you about her first. She's what they call a "German Shepherd." I'm not exactly sure what that means but I know that shepherds like to boss sheep around, so I guess it means that Annie Dog likes to boss Germans around. But there aren't any Germans around on our property, so she tries to boss *us* around instead!

When I first met this feisty furry female, I thought she was pushy and totally annoying, always trying to herd us and barking orders at us in her mixture of English, German and dog language! I once told Annie, "Sammy and I aren't Germans, so stop trying to tell us what to do! Who made *you* the boss, anyway?" She answered, "I know you're not Germans, Dudley. The mom says you llamas are Peruvians. But I'm still your boss because that's just what German Shepherds are, *bosses.* And llamas are *bossees.* You're *MY* responsibility so get used to it!"

For the first two months with my new family I considered Annie Dog *one GIGANTIC pain*! But you know it's funny, isn't it, how sometimes we decide we don't like someone and then later, after we've gotten to know them better, we change our minds about them?

Today I believe that Annie Dog is wise and wonderful and brave and my very best friend in the whole wide world. Now, how's *that* for a big change of heart? I'll explain to you how this change came about later on in my story.

Of course, as the mom always says, "nobody's per-

fect," and neither is Annie. Although she's very kind to people and other animals, including cats, (yuck!), she has a real behavior problem with squirrels.

If the mom isn't looking, this K-9 will give a squirrel a run for its life, although I don't know what she has against these poor, innocent nut collectors.

Next let me tell you about our cats, L.T. and Steamer. Now these two are a pair for you if ever there was one! Always getting themselves into pickles, they often have to be bailed out of trouble by Sammy and Annie and me.

L.T. is your typical female cat, aloof, fin-icky, unpre-dictable, and with a real cat attitude--you know, one minute she likes a scratch and the next minute she doesn't, and if you don't stop annoying her *right that minute* she will hiss at you and threaten you with one of *her* scratches! If you have a girl cat, you probably know what I'm talking about here.

But L.T. is sweet to the people just often enough so that they find her completely charm-ing. HA!

Next we have Mr. Steamer, the boy cat. He's a big, friendly, striped goofy tiger cat who just *loves* people and comes right away when called. In that sense, Steamer is a lot like Sammy, the nose-nuzzling *perfectly pleasant people pleaser.*

Steamer is forever meowing and talking in cat language, which I don't completely understand. He's far too curious and never cautious enough. Does he ever look before he leaps into a jam? No, not our Steamer!

I'll tell you about some of their feline shenanigans later on, but for now, suffice it to say that cats are not as smart as they *think* they are, aloof or not!

Oh, and by the way, in case you don't understand all these fun words I've been using,

"WHO, ME?"

K-9 stands for "canine," which is fancy for dog. *Feline* stands for cat which is fancy for "pest!" And *shenanigans* is a very big word, I know, but it basically just means to get into mischief. I should know about that, expert that I am! So, it's definitely a good word for you to remember if you happen to be a kid. Then if your parents ever ask you what kind of *shenanigans* you're up to, you can just look really innocent and tell them, "Who, me? You must be mistaking me for some other child, one who engages in mischievous activities!" That should throw them off track for a while!

But now, back to the cats. I was telling you about Steamer being far too curious. Actually, llamas are extremely curious animals, too. We llamas have to check out all new things, like what you're wearing, what you're eating, and so on. And when you take our picture with a camera, we'll almost always look straight at the camera, wondering what you're doing. That's why it always looks like we mug for photos. In reality, we don't. We're just being curious.

Of course, I also smile for most of my photos because when people point a camera at me it reminds me of the peek-a-boo game which Claire plays with Sammy, using her blankie. Sammy laughs so hard and acts so silly when Claire plays it with him! And so when people hide their faces behind a camera, I pretend

Smile, Dudley!

they're playing peek-a-boo with me, and I end up with a big smile on my face in the photo. Try imagining this when somebody wants to take your picture, and you'll always take *GREAT* pictures, just like I do!

But back to what I was saying about curiosity. Whenever llamas are curious, we put our ears straight up and facing you. But unlike cats, we do not let our curiosity almost kill us! We have too many brains underneath our big ears to let that happen.

Next up for discussion are the humans. Sammy loves them all equally well, but I happen to prefer the big ones to the little ones.

The little humans, or "kids," as they're called, are usually even worse behaved than our cats! They're always bickering and making mischief and messes and doing things they aren't supposed to do, kind of like me when I lived in the pre-school pasture back at the Rainbow Mountain Llama Ranch.

Now don't get me wrong about this. I know that the children all love Sammy and me very much, and we love them too. But, if the truth be known, kids can be a real *bother* at times!

For instance, let's start with our Christopher. He's ten and he thinks he already knows everything! He always wants to lead me on hikes,

Dudley with Sarah and Annie Dog

but then he wants to stop to investigate insects and other weird stuff, and I have to stand around with my hundred pound packs on, patiently waiting for him to finish with his bugs.

Sometimes Chris takes me out along the irrigation ditch on our property. The water in this ditch comes right out of the Elk River, which is across the road from our property. All sorts of fish and other slimy creatures swim through the ditch, even big, pesky beavers sometimes. He makes me carry his captured fish and frogs and snakes and hoppy things in my pannier bags.

Now, I don't mind carrying weight, and as I've said, I'll even carry over a hundred pounds without complaining, but I don't like what I carry on my back to drip or slither or hop or jump or flop around on me, even if it *is* in a bag. Yuck!

Sarah, who is eight, collects rocks and sticks, among other things. She loads up my panniers with her "specimens" everywhere she goes. Only, she usually puts them all into the same pannier until one side weighs thirty pounds more than the other, and they become unbalanced and slip so badly that the people have to stop to re-cinch my saddle. Then, since kids are always in such a big hurry when they have to do work, Sarah never takes the time to do it right.

A cinch, by the way, is the belt that goes around my belly to hold the saddle on me. It needs to be very tight so that it won't loosen up and cause the saddle and packs to slip around on my back. But when you put a cinch on a llama, you need to take your time and be certain that none of our long hairs get stuck in the buckle. As you can imagine, that really hurts!

So when Sarah doesn't do it correctly, I have to lie down on the trail and refuse to budge for them to finally guess what's wrong, and by

"Get up, Dudley!"

then they're all mad at me again.

"Get up Dudley! For heaven's sake, stop being so independent and stubborn!" they shout at me.

"I'm NOT being stubborn. Thanks to you, hair is caught in my cinch and it hurts. And I'm not going *ANYWHERE* until you figure it out and fix it!"

I hum all of this to them but ,of course, they don't understand me. It's very frustrating for all concerned.

Claire, the "baby caboose" in the family, as she is called, is four. Sometimes they let her ride on my back because she's so little and light. I wouldn't mind this a bit, but she sucks her thumb and is always petting my neck and nose after she pulls her wet thumb out of her mouth. For the record, I don't even like dry fingers on my neck or nose, much less wet ones. Then she squeals into my face, "Duddy Buddy!"

Sarah once showed me a photo of Claire and Sammy taken when they were both toddlers. The family was visiting Sammy when he was still little with his mama. In this photo, Claire is holding her blankie and sucking her thumb, as usual, and Sammy is bugging her to play peek-a-boo with him. It's a real sweet photo, even I have to admit. But if you can imagine it, after she pets my hairy nose, Claire sticks her thumb back into her mouth. Yum, yum, llama hair!

Dudley with Claire

Even when it's cold outside and she's wearing big, fat mittens, Claire will take them off and plop the old thumb in. I always try to nuzzle the back of her neck to make her laugh. She has to take her thumb out to giggle, but then, *plop!* It goes right back in again!

The mom says Claire will stop 'the thumb habit' when she goes to kindergarten, but I'll believe *that* when I see it!

One final kid thing that drives me batty is that they sing a llama song which my writer friend put in the back of this book, against my wishes. My humans sing it over and over to us on the trail, and it drives me stir crazy!

Now don't get me wrong. There's absolutely nothing wrong with lloving a llama. In fact, it's pretty hard *NOT* to llove a llama, if you

Toddlers, Claire & Sammy

ask me. But hearing that song over and over is far worse than *100 Bottles of Beer on the Wall,* which is another annoying song they sing until the mom makes them stop. Unfortunately, the mom likes the llama song, no matter how many times they sing it!

Sammy, naturally, loves the song and hums right along with them. I heard somebody tell my writer friend that it's a "real nifty song," so I guess the word nifty means *annoying!*

The people mom is pretty nice to all of us animals, although she often babytalks to us. Yuck! Sammy and Steamer like it, but L.T. and I don't go in for that kind of stuff. I'm *not* a baby anymore, and it drives me bananas when she says, "Hi there Bubbly Dudley! How 'ya doin' sweetie pie?" It's almost enough to make me spit up!

The baby-talker mom is also pretty good at understanding animal talk and posturing. She almost always seems to know what I'm thinking, even when I wish she didn't. Annie Dog and the mom understand each other pretty well, too. For some reason, though, it's hard for the mom to communicate with her own human children and she's always asking them, "Why is it that everything I tell you children just goes in one ear and out the other?"

Sometime I think humans are stranger than fiction!

As for the dad, he's usually O.K., except when he tells the mom, "Don't go so easy on the llamas. You need to treat them more like beasts of burden and less like pets and they'll behave better for you, *especially Dudley*!" Quote, unquote. Can you believe that?

This dad certainly doesn't understand my need to be independent, and he's always trying to show me he's the boss. Sammy, of course, doesn't make it any easier for me by doing everything he's told to do as soon as he's told to do it. "Yes, sir. Right away, sir!"

Sometimes when Sammy acts like this, *PATOOIE*! I just have to spit at him. I can't help myself. But I never spit at him in front of the dad anymore. You see, the last time I did, the dad got really angry at me. He walked over to me and spat right in *my* face! I was shocked. Then he yelled at me, "*STOP SPITTING AT YOUR BROTHER, DUDLEY!* Do you like getting a taste of your own medicine, mister?"

Talk about overreacting!!

I knew enough not to spit back at him. We well-bred llamas are supposed to spit only at our own kind, *never* at people, if we know what's good for us! So now I try to spit at Sammy only when the people aren't around, especially the dad. I don't relish (or catsup) getting spat back at. Hey, that's a pretty good rhyme for a poem. Let's see...

Watch out for me,
I'm Dead-Eye Dudley.
My aim is superb,
and I'm not at all cuddly.
Other llamas complain
I'm a spitting brat,
For I never abide
Getting spat back at.
For, in spitting
I follow one rule, you see,
" 'Tis far better to give
than receive," says me!

CHAPTER 3

LIFE IN THE ROCKIES

AND MORE LLAMA

LLORE

I f you've never spent time in the Rocky Mountains, you should try it sometime, especially in the summer. Life out here is "pretty glorious," as the mom calls it. The world looks so beautiful from our pasture. The Colorado sky is almost always a dark blue, the clouds are big, fluffy, and white, the wildflowers are spectacular in color and utterly delicious in taste, and the sun shines part of almost every single day of the year here. Rocky Mountain air is clean and dry and cool, and there are zillions of terrific hiking trails that take us high into the mountains, even up to peaks in the Mt. Zirkel Wilderness area which are more than 10,000 feet high. That's almost two miles up in the sky. Have you ever been that high up and still had your feet on the ground? If not, you should try it some day. The great feeling it will give you is called a "Rocky Mountain High."

"Trailhead" is what they call the place where a hiking trail actually begins, and the trailheads for many of these hiking trails are almost in our back yard. When I first heard that expression, I thought it meant that there were going to be all sorts of heads rolling around on the trails--decapitated people heads and animal heads of all varieties. *Yikes!* So I was greatly relieved to learn otherwise.

My brother and I walk on these trails all the

time except in the winter when the snow's too deep for us to walk through. In winter, some people attach wide, flat tennis rackets to their real feet. The tennis rackets spread the weight out over the snow so that people don't sink down into it, and then they're able to walk on top of deep snow. They call these special tennis rackets "snowshoes."

Snowshoe Person

Snowshoe Rabbit

I'd really like to try walking on snowshoes myself, but as far as I know, they only make them now for people and for rabbits.

I do get to pull a sleigh up and down Seedhouse Road in the winter, and that's sleds of fun. Poor Claire has to sit inside of the sleigh, totally bundled up in scarves and a warm goose feather quilt. (Honk! Honk!) I can't even see her face. Then the other humans in my family put funny boards on their feet called "cross-country skis," and they glide along in front of me on the snow-packed road. On very cold, sunny days, for some reason they wear disguises on their faces -- dark eyes and scarves.

Weird bunch, my family!

Annie Dog gets to go almost everywhere with the mom, even in the car. That's why she knows so much about the world and about human beings. Well, that and also from watching the T.V. machine in the people house.

She also gets to go with us on every hike,

but fortunately, they leave the two cats at home. L.T. and Steamer manage to get into quite enough trouble without ever leaving our property. If they came along with us into the wilderness, they'd no doubt get lost or soon be eaten by a coyote.

Hmmm, now perhaps that's not such a bad idea? "Here kitty, kitty. Want to come on our hike with us? Heh, heh, just kidding, kitty."

When Sammy and I were little, the people put small packs on us and walked us all around the property. They told us we were being trained to be "pack animals." Now there's that expression again. As we grew bigger and stronger, our packs got bigger and heavier, and eventually we discovered that "pack animals" really means "slave laborers."

But I usually don't mind carrying the packs, though. I'm strong and hardy and have big muscles in my back and legs, but Sammy minds. Of course, he doesn't complain to the family, only to me.

My favorite hikes are in the late spring when we go out with just the mom and Annie Dog. The mom says that we all need to lose our winter fat, especially she and Sammy, and so we hike fast and far all day long. Usually there's still some snow and mud up on the higher trails and we get to tramp through all of that, too.

We sound really great! *Squish, squash, splish, splash, slip, slop!* Try to say that ten times really fast!

Sammy hates to walk in mud and deep

snow, though, and he complains, "You know I don't like to put my feet down into things that make them cold or dirty!" Then he hums one of his complaining hums, "Hum, hum, where's the ground? Hum, hum, where's the trail? Hum, hum, now my feet are all cold and wet! Hum, hum, oh bother!"

When we're around patches of snow on the trail, I always remind Sammy, also known as "Mr. Gullible," to look out for the snowsnakes, and that gets him all riled up too. You see, snowsnakes are just imaginary snakes, but I always forget to tell Sammy that part of it. Heh, heh.

About once a week, a hot air balloon drifts right over our property carrying guests from a nearby tourist ranch. For the longest time, I had Sammy believing that it was a gigantic round, flame-spitting, llama-eating bird. But then one landed right in our pasture once, and Sammy saw *people* inside the basket! When he looked at me with a questioning look, I just started to hum my *innocent* hum, "Hum de dum dum hum hum hum."

When a llama's happy, he or she says, "Hum, hum, hum." When a llama's sad, it's usually, "Oh hum, oh hum." When we're bored we say, "Ho Hum," and when llamas are worried, upset or angry about something, it's *"HOLY HUM HUM!!!!!"*

When we llamas spot danger, we let out a loud, high-pitched, ear-piercing HOLY HUM HUM whine to warn you, "like a fire truck," says Christopher. Most people get all our regular hums mixed up, but they always seem to know what we mean when we whine out that shrill warning signal.

When male llamas in herds fight, they try to scare each another with very loud, frightening screams. And then they crash up against each other, too. But Sammy and I never fight that way,

44

thank goodness, since we're much too civilized! Besides, Sammy usually just lets me be the leader anyway, so there's not too much for us to fight about.

For some reason, people like to hum back to us on the trail, and so they often imitate our hums. But if they only knew some of the things they were actually humming, they would be greatly embarrassed!

For instance, sometimes I hum out, "Boy, these people are acting like nit-wits today!" Then, one of the people imitates my hum, thinking he's being very clever, without knowing what he's just said.

I, for one, laugh until my saddle cinch hurts, but Mr. Goody-Two-Shoes reminds me, "You shouldn't make fun of the humans that way, Dudley. It's unkind!" I tell him, "Lighten up, bro, and I'm *NOT* referring to the weight of your packs!"

Besides not liking to walk in deep snow, Sammy also doesn't enjoy crossing cold streams. Now, I don't mind this myself because, like most llamas, if the people let me, I like to stop every now and then for a good long cold drink.

Speaking of long drinks, as you probably know, llamas are very distant cousins of the camel, both of us belonging to the camelid family of animals. But llamas look, smell and act far better than camels, and we don't have that strange hump. We're smaller than camels, but we both have long necks and soft, leathery pads on the bottom of our feet. We also both have large eyes with long, protecting lashes, and skinny heads. And like camels, we have a split upper lip and three sections in our stomachs, which I'll tell you about later when I explain to you about spitting cud.

And llamas have far better dispositions than camels, no doubt about that! If you don't believe me about llamas looking, acting and smelling better than camels, just go to a zoo and somehow get yourself up close to a camel. Try to get near enough to get a good whiff of him, and then be ready to hold your nose and run, because the smelliest of the mammals are the cabbage head camels! And they often spit at people, too!

Camels can store water for a lot longer period than we llamas, but we don't have to drink as often as most other animals. When we finally do take a drink, we usually make it an extremely *long* drink. Annie says it reminds her of when the people give cars and trucks their drinks, using long hoses connected to pumps.

Annie once told me, "I just love to watch you llamas drink from a bucket, Dudley. Somehow you suck up the water so fast and quietly, it almost looks like you're using a straw. Really neat! How do you do that? I wish I could drink like that."

If you have a dog, you know about the disgusting way they drink--lapping up water with their tongues, splashing it everywhere and making big wet sloppy messes on the floor and impolite slurping noises. Yuck!

I feel sorry for poor Annie Dog when she does that, and I don't make fun of her about it because that's just the way God made dogs, poor things.

Now, cats are much neater drinkers and eaters than dogs, and they like to keep themselves very clean. But they do it by licking themselves with their own spit! Isn't that disgusting? I use spit, too, but not to make anything clean. Quite the opposite, if you get my drift!

But back to hiking in the Rockies. That's how this llama book idea got started in the first place, on a hike in the Rockies.

Actually, it was on a hike up Notch Mountain, a trail near Vail, Colorado. This hiking trail is about five miles long to the top, and it climbs almost 3,000 feet in elevation. That means that when you finally stand on the top of this mountain, you're almost two and a half miles (13,100 feet) higher up in the sky than when you're sitting on a beach at the ocean, which is called "sea level." Up at this high altitude there's less oxygen to breathe, and so it can be a pretty difficult hike for most people to make, but not for us llamas.

At high altitudes and harsh environments, llamas have an easier time of it than humans because we have enlarged lungs which take in more oxygen, and we also have more red blood cells which carry the oxygen faster to all parts of our bodies.

Llamas also have very big hearts, hardy backs and strong legs, all of which make hiking and carrying weight much easier for us than it is for humans.

We can't be ridden like horses, but we can carry all of your camping and hiking supplies. And unlike horses, we have lots of common sense and are very steady and sure-footed on the kinds of steep, rocky trials and slippery sliding slopes found in the Rocky Mountains.

So, on this particular hike up Notch Mountain, Sammy and I and four other llamas were brought along to help people in this church group carry all the things they needed for their trip, like food and water, a first aid kit, warm clothes for the windy top, a backpacker guitar, camera equipment, and so on.

Using llamas as pack animals like this began about 6,000 years ago in Peru, a very mountainous country in South America where they use llamas to transport things to places where cars and trucks can't easily go.

In South America, after a llama gets old and worn out from working hard for people, they usually slaughter him and use his meat for food and his hide for shelters and sandals. How's *that* for gratitude! The mom says that the people there are sort of poor and that they have to do that, but I'm just glad that Sammy and I don't live down there. In fact, I don't even want us to *ever* visit South America, especially after we get old and retire. *YIKES!*

Back to the Notch Mountain trip, though. This is where I first met my author friend, the human who wrote these stories down for me.

At the time, she says she had hiked for many years and had seen people hiking with llamas, but that she personally had never spent any time around llamas. I guess she just didn't know what she was missing!

When my owners asked her that day if she'd like to lead me on the trail, she almost said no. She was afraid that having a llama tagging along behind her would slow her down. And besides, she added, "Don't llamas spit at people?"

"No, Dudley is a well-bred llama, and he only spits at other animals, usually at his poor, innocent brother!" Then the dad glowered at me.

The author lady looked dubiously at me, but I smiled and blinked my large, intelligent-looking eyes at her a few times--like this, blink, blink, blink -- and that charmed her into saying "yes," that she would lead me. She also later told me that my eyes had "a bit of a twinkle to them," and that this had led her to believe that I might be a fun fellow to be around.

She was right! *Fun* should be my middle name.

Soon after we started to hike, the lady discovered that I not only didn't slow her down, but that this "strange-looking creature" was willing and able to go at any pace she set and could have easily left her far behind had I not been trained to mind my manners and stay behind her.

Even more than my speed, however, she said that I had surprised her with my constant humming. Trying to get her attention, I made my hums go way up and down in pitch during the whole trip up and during the whole trip back down. She soon realized that I wasn't singing to her, but that I was trying to communicate with her.

"What do you think he's trying to tell me?" she asked my owners. But even they didn't give her the correct answer.

"Is he complaining that I'm not going fast enough for him? Or do you think he's just upset because we're hiking faster than his buddies?" She had heard that we llamas like to stick around with each other on the trail, but since she and I were such fast hikers, we'd left the others behind in our wake, so to say.

One human told her wrongly that I was probably just complaining about all of the *switchbacks* on the trail, the part of a hiking trail which travels back and forth across a mountain like a continuing 'Z'. It's much easier to climb this more gradual way up and down rather than straight up and down, especially on the very steep sections of a trail.

On the Notch Mountain trail, especially near the top, there are numerous switchbacks going back and forth, back and forth, making hikers dizzy. But, no, that wasn't what I had been trying to tell her that day.

From the top of Notch Mountain, you can look over at the top of the adjacent mountain peak, which is called Mount of the Holy Cross. This very famous peak in Colorado is yet another thousand feet higher than the top of Notch

Mount of the Holy Cross, as seen from atop Notch Mountain
Mountain climbers are on top of the peak.

Mountain, and it looks so close that you feel like you can almost reach out and touch it with your hoof or your hand. But you're really much further away than that, and there's a deep chasm between you and that other peak.

On the side of the Holy Cross Mountain which faces you when you sit on the top of Notch Mountain, you can see a famous huge cross of snow, even in the middle of the summer. It's quite an impressive sight, and as my author friend explained to the people how this cross got to be there, she noticed that I was watching her, trying to understand her explanation.

She told us that there are two very long, twenty-five to fifty feet deep ditches in the rock which cross each other. The up and down, vertical ditch is 1,500 feet long, and the horizontal ditch which crosses it is 750 feet long. During winter snowstorms, these deep ditches fill up with snow and that snow then remains long after the shallow snow around it melts, thus, leaving the large white cross standing out against the darker surrounding rocks. Other patches of snow remain in various places, too, making it look like someone painted on the side of the mountain with white paint.

"What a boring explanation!," I thought. So, I went over to the other five llamas who were resting away from the people, and I spruced the story up a bit to make it more interesting for them. I told them to look down into the chasm to see the *Humongous Cross-Country Ski Giant!* It was *HE* who had painted the cross and other white marks on the side of the mountain ahead of them, and this crazed creature was still clumping around on the rocks on gigantic cross-country skis, looking for animals and people to squish and paint X's and crosses on!

I described this imaginary giant so well that they thought they really saw him, when actually they were looking at a big old spruce tree down the mountain. *HA!* They got all nervous and worried and riled up, and their knees wobbled. The people couldn't understand what had spooked the llamas or why they were humming nervous hums.

Me? I just stood there smiling and

humming an *innocent* hum.

A few weeks after our Notch Mountain trip, my author friend came to visit us at our home in Clark, and she took Sammy and me out on many hikes and overnight trips. She was curious to see if I had really been trying to communicate with her, as indeed I was! So, I hummed to her as much as I could.

Finally, she started to ask me specific

questions and then paid very close attention to my replies. When she began to listen to me more with her eyes and her heart, it all began to make sense to her. For you see, besides our humming, we llamas also communicate with our body posturing and by the various ways we can hold our ears and our tails.

So *HALLELUJAH AND HOLY HUM HUM!!* A person could now communicate with a llama, and *I* was that llucky llama!

I had so very much to tell her, so I hummed almost non-stop from then on. For starters I explained to her that on our first hike together, I had heard somebody say that she had written a book. Since I wanted to write a book myself but couldn't, I decided to try to get her to help me do it.

"Now, why does a llama want to write a book?" you might wonder. Well, I want to write a book about *llamas.* I want people to know more about us than simply the facts that we like to hum and spit at each other. I want people to know that, in addition to those two things, we llamas are extraordinary animals--very intelligent, alert, curious, independent, playful, charming, strong, shy, obedient (usually!), meek, fun-loving, hard working, gentle, calm, clean, easy to care for, easily-trained and, of course, very humble. In short, we are the perfect all-around family pet, although I prefer to be called a "family companion" myself.

Oh, and I almost forgot, once we're trained how to do something, we almost *never* forget it, and we also have fantastic eyesight. If you ever see us gazing far off into the distance at something, you should try to follow our gaze. We're most likely looking at something very interesting like a deer or an elk or a cross-country ski giant which you would otherwise be sure to miss with your limited people vision.

Sammy, on the other hand, is usually more interested in what the people are doing and what's right ahead of him, and he's forever asking me what I'm looking up at. I tell him, "I'm looking at pretty llama girls in the sky, Sam." He looks up, but he never sees them, poor guy!

Unfortunately, our great eyesight didn't help Sammy and me even one little bit when we managed to get ourselves totally lost in the wilderness once. But that's yet another long story to tell.

Oh, You Gotta' Llove a Llama!

CHAPTER 4

THE ADVENTURES BEGIN
-LOST IN THE WILDERNESS-

During my first autumn with my family, on a special day they call "Thanks-and-Forgiving Day," one of the children--I won't tell you which since I'm not a snitch--left the gate of our pasture fence open. Later on, long after this adventure I'm about to relate to you was over, the dad said to this guilty child, "I guess you must have been just trying to act like a turkey on Thanks-and-Forgiving Day when you left that gate open!"

I knew that the gate probably wasn't supposed to be left open, special day or not, but I for one never look a gift horse in the mouth, mainly because horses have very bad breath.

Anyway, being only two years old and not yet blessed with an overabundance of good judgement, I decided to take this gift of an open gate and go out into the big world for a while to do a little exploring--*without* supervision.

Of course, I didn't want to go out totally on my own, not without my buddy, Sammy. Since llamas don't like to go anywhere without a buddy llama, I told Sammy, "Come on with me, bro! We'll get back home before they even miss us!"

Mr. Perfect Llama said, "No way, Dudley! You know very well that we aren't supposed to go anywhere without people supervision. That would be disobedient!"

"Chill out, Sammy! Loosen up and come join the fun. We won't stay out too long. I promise you we'll be back before dark, O.K.?" Still no dice. Mr. Goody-Two-Shoes wasn't budging.

So I called him a chicken and a few other terribly nasty names. The poor guy *finally* lost his temper, and he puckered up for a good spit. But, of course, his conscience got the best of him, and he stopped himself just in the nick of time. Good thing, too, because I had my ears way back on my head, all puckered up for a good spit back, and I'm a much better aim than Sammy is since he almost never spits. I had only seen him spit once before, at an annoying fly, and naturally he had missed.

Finally, my nagging and intimidation wore him down, and just to shut me up and against his better judgment, Sammy finally gave in and said, "All right, Dudley, I'll go along to get along. But remember, we get back here before dark. You promise!"

So out the open gate we went, my buddy and I, off to explore the big world!

By the way, I must tell you that if you're ever standing next to a llama and he puts his ears way back on his head, move far away from him. Quick! He's getting ready to spit, and even if it's only at another llama, many llamas don't have accurate aims like me, Dead-Eye Dudley!

Luckily--or unluckily as it turned out-- nobody saw us leave, and we snuck quietly down the driveway, turned left off of our land, and then headed up Seedhouse Road along the Elk River for about a mile. A few cars passed us, but I told Sam to act like we knew what we were doing, and so nobody stopped to see what two *ll*ose *ll*amas were up to.

Then, off to the left, we saw an interesting little trail which leads up to Farwell Mountain, although we didn't know this at the time. It looked pretty inviting, so we followed it uphill, munching wonderfully-tasting barks off of different kinds of trees and bushes. "What a nice variety for a change," I mentioned to Sammy. "Yes, *crunch, crunch,*" he replied, "this sure is savory high fiber. Maybe this wasn't such a bad idea after all, Dudsey. *Crunch, crunch.* I'm certainly having a delightfully delicious out time here, in spite of having to walk in this slushy snow!"

Aspen Leaves

Unfortunately, we had just missed the tasty, tender aspen leaves. A few weeks before, they were still on the trees, first green, and then eventually golden and red and shimmering in the sun. That's why they call them "quaking aspen," because they sort of shake and wiggle in the breeze. But now they were all dead on the ground, brown and black and rotting in the early snow.

"What a waste!" I thought. "Oh well, there's always next year's crop of leaves to look forward to."

As we happily continued our trail munching, I remarked to Sammy, "Yes, bro, you should listen to me more often. This trip is definitely one of my better ideas, isn't it?"

But no sooner had I hummed these words than the sky began to darken, the wind began to howl, and hard, frozen ice balls called "hailstones" began to pelt us in the face.

"Ouch! Ouch! Ouch!," Sammy wailed. "What's happening, Dudley? Somebody's throwing stones at us! And it's getting dark out already. Ouch! I don't like this one bit! Ouch, ouch! Let's go home right now! You promised!"

A big streak of lightning shot out across the sky, and a loud thunder boom soon followed in the distance.

K a b o o m!!!

Sammy, nearing panic, wailed, "Dudley, let's get home to our barn *RIGHT NOW!* Don't you know that llamas are required to be inside of barns during all lightning storms?"

"Calm down, Sammy. I've never heard of *that* rule. I think you just made it up! What nonsense! Just follow me now. I think the trail is right over here. Or is it over in that direction? Hmmm. Now, let me think..."

But before I was able to locate the trail, yet another bolt of bright lightning crackled overhead, and an extremely loud boom exploded right next to us.

K A B O O M!!

This time Sammy immediately shrilled his alarm and bolted off in a fast run. Unfortunately, he didn't even try to find the trail but raced wildly about, crashing through trees and meadows of slush.

By the time I caught up with him and managed to stop him, we had absolutely *no* idea where the trail might be.

"Whoa bro! Calm down, will ya? Let's just stay cool and use our brains. Now, where do you think they might put a trail around here?"

We wandered around together for a long time, searching for the lost trail, but to no avail. It was impossible to follow our own hoof marks since there were also hundreds of hoof marks left behind by a herd of some other animal.

And eventually, even I, brave llama that I am, began to worry. Would we keep walking in circles forever, lost in the wilderness? "Poor, poor us. Poor, poor lost llamas!"

After a while, though, as quickly as it had all started, the wind, freezing rain and hail all stopped, and a little bit of the sun began to peek out through the clouds. I could see a beautiful rainbow on the top of a nearby mountain, and it reminded me of the place where I was born, the Rainbow Mountain Llama Ranch. I suddenly remembered my mama llama, and oh, how I wished I was with her right then!

Sammy hummed, "Why did I *ever* listen to you, Dudley?" Then he cried terribly llarge llama tears, and I felt so guilty for having taunted him into coming with me on this disastrous misadventure. Poor Sammy. What had I done to him? What had I done to *US*?

And then, as if things couldn't get any worse, we suddenly heard several other big booms, but they weren't like the lightning booms.

BOOM! BOOM! they sounded, one right after the other, and pretty close by, too!

Then, crashing out of the trees and bushes came a humongous brown animal. It was as big as a horse, but this for certain wasn't a horse. I knew the horses in the neighboring pasture, and they were tall and huge, too, but they never had five-foot-across racks of horns on the tops of their heads! Weird!

Plus, I got a whiff of its smell, and it was worse than stinky horse odor!

I figured that whatever this huge monster was, with its long legs, it could easily catch us if we tried to run away.

So I whispered to Sammy, "Calm down, brother. Try to stand still and don't let him know you're afraid!"

Amazingly, Sammy listened to me and remained standing there, swaying nervously from foot to foot, humming a fast, loud, worried hum. "So much for showing no fear, Sammy!" I thought to myself! "Oh well..."

The giant animal looked us over, and then asked us, in a real snobby sort of way, "Whatever kind of foolish-looking animals are you two? Certainly not majestic bull elks like me, and you hum little nervous hums instead of bugle. How unimpressive! Oh, and by the way, you both look and smell quite badly, too -- P.U.!"

Just as I was about to tell this high-and-mighty wapiti how badly *HE* looked and smelled, we heard another big *BOOM!!* and Mr. Big Shot took off running. As he did, though, he barked back to us, "You'd better watch out for the hunters! They're all around here, and they won't be able to miss you two weird birds!"

"Birds?" Did he call us birds? What nerve!

I called out after him, "For your information, buster, we're llamas, two *l*'s, two *a*'s, an *m* and an *s*, although not exactly in that order!" But he was long gone by the time I got all of those letters out of my mouth.

How pathetic! There we were, my buddy and I, two weird birds out all alone, lost in the woods, surrounded by hunters, although we weren't too sure what hunters even were! We figured that these hunters probably had something to do with the frightening booms, and my instinct told me we shouldn't be anywhere near them *or* their booms.

But how could we escape from them? Where was the trail? Where was Seedhouse Road and our property and our warm barn and our family...? Large, wet snowflakes began to fill the cold air, swirling around us, thicker and thicker. The ground began to quickly turn more solidly white, and Sammy the white llama became harder and harder to see. "Just what we need!" I thought.

"Now we'll never, *EVER* find the trail," I said to myself in quiet despair. "What had I done to us? This was *supposed* to be a great adventure, not a great *disaster*!!"

Soon, about a half-inch layer of white wet snow had piled atop Sammy's head. Under normal circumstances, I would have laughed at such a silly sight, but somehow at this point, I didn't think it was so funny. Instead, I felt just terrible because I had made my brother so afraid and unhappy. *"He's a good guy, and he certainly doesn't deserve this, Dudley, you jerk!,"* I scolded myself.

He was sobbing big tears and telling me we were probably being punished for disobedience. I almost joined him in a good cry. The tears came so close to falling, from about here...to here. But just as my warm teardrops threatened to mix with the cold snowflakes, I heard a dog's barking, and it wasn't just any old dog's barking. I recognized this German-English barking, and it was beautiful music to my ears. My heart started to race, and I hummed a joyful hum.

"It's her, Sammy! I know it is! It's just got to be her!"

And then suddenly, she was there, right in front of us, all hot and bothered and scolding us in German, English and dog language, all mixed together. Sweet, wonderful Annie! What a sight for sore eyes!

"We're saved, Sammy, we're saved! Annie Dog has found us!"

"BAD LLAMAS! Where have you been? You get home this minute! Out here all by yourselves with that 800 pound bugling elk.... and the hunters..... and the snowstorm! Get moving, you turkeys!

"Turn right! Now turn left. Move it, you banana-eared boneheads! Move it! Hurry it up, you two mush-for-brains beasts!"

She scolded us like this for the whole, entire way home, nipping at our legs from time to time to encourage us to run even faster whenever we'd hear yet another couple of those hunter booms.

"All right! All right! Sorry, Annie. We're going as fast as we can. We'll never do anything like this again, we promise. Ouch! Ouch! Don't nip my leg! All right already!"

She soon had us back on the snow-covered trail and heading down to good old Seedhouse Road and then home sweet home! First a right turn onto the road, and then back onto our property and happiness, happiness!

When the angry dog marched us all the way up to the big house and barked at the door, everyone, including the nosy cats, poured out the door and into the snowstorm to greet us.

The dad wasn't there because he was still out looking for us, his "naughty runaway llamas," as Sarah called us. But the mom and the children were so joyful to see us back safely that they even forgot to scold us. They left that job up to Annie, who continued to do it with great gusto!

Still seethingly angry at us, she growled her low German Shepherd growl and showed us her sharp, white teeth for the next half hour or so.

"We're sorry, Annie! Really. Why are you so upset with us?"

When she finally calmed down a bit, Annie explained to us about guns and hunters and hunting season, and we suddenly understood her great anger with us. We could have ended up as llama rugs in front of some hunter's fireplace!

"You two should thank God those hunters got skunked today, at least as far as llamas go," Annie chastised us.

I for one was very happy to hear that the mean llama hunters had gotten skunked! "Serves them right!" I thought.

69

Now, I'm sure that Sammy and I would make beautiful llama rugs, but what dummy would want to spend the rest of their time on this earth as a quiet, old boring rug?

And then Annie reminded us that she herself could have been shot, too, out there looking for us. And the dad might *still* be in danger, she added. "For shame, you two, for shame!"

Sammy and I hung our heads way down low. A look of guilt oozed out of my eyes, and Sammy said he felt "so ashamed."

"Sorry, bro. I didn't mean to get us into so much trouble."

The mom hugged Annie and told her how "smart and wonderful and brave" she was. Annie licked her face as a thank you--yuck. But the mom was right about Annie's bravery, that's for sure!

70

The children hugged Sammy and my necks really hard, and Sammy nose-nuzzled them back. I suddenly understood why they call this Thanks-and-Forgiving Day!

I pretended not to like the hugging, but actually, I was so happy just to be alive that it didn't feel all that bad. Sarah and Claire kept kissing me, and I figured that this was punishment enough for me, although I don't think they meant it to be!

Later, when the dad was safely home, he brought the children down to our pasture gate and gave them a lesson in opening and closing it. The infamous turkey child had to open and close the gate thirty times, in three sets of ten.

"How come I always get blamed for everything?," wailed the guilty child, protesting his/her innocence. "*HA!* You fibber!," I hummed.

Sammy stood there the whole time watching, thinking it was some sort of a counting game. Now he's really great at counting up to ten.

Me? Well, I just quietly and carefully observed, and now I know how the gate opens and closes. But don't worry. I won't ever use this knowledge unless there's a real emergency. I figure I had learned my lesson that day about taking off on my own, and thanks to Annie Dog, I'm still here to tell you this tale.

I looked over at her standing loyally at the dad's side, wagging her tail. "She's so smart and so brave," I thought. "Who would have ever guessed?"

Now on any given day, most llamas are smarter than most dogs, and we don't bite, dig holes or have fleas, either. But *this* dog is even smarter than two smart llamas put together, and then some! And I will never, ever, spit at her, not in a gazillion years!

Of course, I didn't say that I would always mind her, just that I wouldn't spit at her. There's a difference.

* * * * * *

As fate would have it, the following summer a whole herd of those snobby, arrogant elk came through our property, completely uninvited. They easily jumped right over the property fence and then headed for the mom's vegetable garden.

Then they hopped over the high garden fence, too, just like it wasn't even there, and they started to nibble away at the mom's good veggies- -*munch, munch, munch.*

Well, I wasn't about to stand for that!

"Just who do those brown bozo buglers think they are? What nerve!," I raved to Sammy. So we joined forces, and together we let out the loudest, shrillest llama alarm we could muster up.

A L A R M !! A L A R M !! ELK IN THE GARDEN. ALARM! ALARM!

It worked! Annie Dog heard our warning all the way up at the big house. Racing to the vegetable garden, the angry canine gave those snobby elk a piece of her mind and a piece of our mind, too!

"You tell 'em, Annie, you tell 'em, girl!!"

Then the mom came outside to investigate. With legs a-running and arms a-flailing, she chased all of the remaining smelly beasts off our property. And people think we *llamas* act berserk!

"Get out of my vegetable garden, you big lummoxes! Now get!"

"You tell 'em, mom, you tell 'em! HA!"

As they ran past our pasture, I hummed out loudly to them, "Good riddance, all you strange-looking, rack-headed weird birds!!"   So I had gotten in the last word after all! Hurray for me!

Now, I suppose I probably should tell you about the time Sammy and I got caught in the mom's vegetable garden, but it's actually a pretty embarrassing story. So, let's just say that it happened once and it won't happen again, if you know what I mean.

But even getting caught red-hooved in the berserk mom's veggie garden wasn't nearly as embarrassing as becoming frightened by your own ghost, the next tale in this book. I come out looking like a real silly goose in it, so I know you won't want to miss it!

* * * * * *

CHAPTER 5

THE GHOST LLAMA

Once when Sammy and I were pretty new at being pack animals, the people were putting saddles on us for a trip. They always try to saddle us before we leave our home to save time at the trailhead. If our saddles are already on us when we arrive, then our people just have to attach the pannier bags to the saddles, and we can begin our hike. If they leave the saddle cinching for the trailhead, strangers always have time to come over and ask my owners a thousand questions about llamas, and then we're late in starting our hike.

These strangers always seem to ask the same questions over and over again, both at the trailhead and also while we're hiking on the trail, so to keep us from getting bored from hearing the same old answers, I hum out some more creative answers than those my owners give. For instance:

Stranger: "Hi, what are these guys? Little camels?"

Dad: "Oh no, they're called llamas."

Me: "Camels? Boy, are you a genius! You see any humps on me?"

Stranger: "Oh, llamas. Of course, that's what I meant. Don't llamas spit at people?"

Dad: "Well, not the trained ones. Our llamas only spit at other llamas pretty much. We train them carefully."

Me: "Spit at people? Why, yes we do. Would you like a demonstration?"

Stranger: "Is it usual for a llama to be all white like that one?

Dad: Yes it's very common, but llamas come in all sorts of solids and mixtures of whites, browns, blacks, grays, beige, reds and roans. Dudley's markings are very typical. Some are spotted and marked in pretty patterns like that.

Me: "I do have a purple and orange llama cousin, but he went up the other trail. Why don't you go look for him!"

Stranger: "How much do they weigh?"

Dad: "Oh, anywhere between 250 and 400 pounds."

Me: "On a fat day, about a gabillion pounds!"

Stranger: "What do they eat?"

Dad: "Mostly just grass, and once in a while, a little oats."

Me: "What do we eat? Why, people who ask too many questions, for a starter. And then rocky trail ice cream cones for dessert."

Stranger: "Can you ride on them?"

Dad: "Well, little children under seventy pounds can, if the llama's trained for it. And they can be trained to pull sleds and carts, too, but we generally just use these guys for packing."

Me: "You try to ride on me buster, and I'll dump you on the ground lickety-split, head over-heels, and out to lunch you go!"

Stranger: "Aren't there other kinds of llamas, sort of smaller and skinnier ones than this fat kind?"

Dad: "Yes, there are other smaller lamoids, and they're called wild guanaco, vicuna and alpaca which is usually raised just for its wool. Most of these lamoids live in South America. Our llamas here stand about five-foot-six, from hoof to head tops."

Me: "Fat kind? You think we're the *FAT* kind? Well, I'd rather be *fat* than stupid!"

Now these question askers might not understand my answers, but I think they're much more creative than the same old polite, boring replies which my owners patiently repeat over and over. So, they're getting the right information, but Sammy and I and Annie already know the answers, and it's fun to try to come up with new ones every time.

On this particular day, when we were still at home getting saddled, they finished mine and started to work on Sammy's, but they forgot to tie my lead rope to the trailer. Never one to look a gift horse in the mouth, remember, I moseyed around to the front of the big blue truck. As I did this, I was surprised to see another llama looking at me from inside of the truck.

"Well I'll be! *Who* is *that*? He's sure a handsome fellow! How'd he get inside the truck like that?"

When I moved closer to the window to check him out, he disappeared. I moseyed on over to the other side of the truck, looked in that window, and there he was again. The same thing happened--when I got close to the window and peeked into the truck, he disappeared.

"Hey, what kind of a llama *are* you anyway? A magical llama? A Houdini llama? A one-L Dalai Lama? A ghost llama? Wait a minute, did I just say *GHOST LLAMA*? That *had* to be it! *A GHOST LLAMA!* Why, sure! *WHOA! I'M OUTA' HERE!!!*"

With that, I took off in a fast run for the barn, with various family members and Annie Dog in hot pursuit behind me. The bossy K-9 finally caught up to me, grabbing my lead

in her mouth and pulling on it sharply to stop me. "Halt!" she barked in German. "Stop!"

When she asked me what had happened, I told her about the ghost llama inside the truck.

Annie wagged her tail and laughed her annoying German Shepherd laugh, which sounds a lot like she's trying to cough up something that is stuck in her throat.

"Stop laughing at me, Annie! It's not funny! I saw a ghost llama, I tell you!"

"You didn't see a ghost, you silly goose! You just saw your own reflection in the window!"

Then she patiently explained to me about reflections, and I did feel like a silly goose, or at least a silly mongoose!

When the people took me back to the trailer, I snuck another look in the truck window, and by golly, it *was* me!

"Wow! So that's what I look like? Far out! Brown with white on my forehead and on the front of my neck, just like my mama! "Not bad, Dashing Dudley Dude, not bad!," I hummed.

When they put Sammy and me into the trailer, I couldn't resist playing a little trick on him. When he asked me why I'd run away before, I told him I'd seen a scary white ghost llama in the truck window. As always, Mr. Gullible believed me and acted nervous and concerned.

When they unloaded us, I dared Sammy, "Go take a look for yourself, bro."

He wouldn't, of course. But a few minutes later, when he wasn't thinking about it, one of the children happened to lead Sammy past the front of the truck when he wasn't paying attention, and he glanced at the window before he realized what he was doing. There it was, the scary white ghost llama!

By the way, as you must know by now, Sammy is a white llama. Well, he let out a horrible llama alarm and started to jump up and kick at the air and pull away from the child's hold.

Nobody could figure out what had happened, and that particular child got scolded, "You must have done something terrible to him to spook Sammy like that! What did you do?"

"Nothing, Dad, I promise!"

You see, unlike horses, we llamas are not easily spooked. Llamas usually have calm and predictable responses to new situations. So Sammy getting spooked was very unusual behavior for a llama, even for Sammy.

Naturally, they would never think it was Sammy's fault, since he's so *perfect.* It had to have been something the child did to him, the parents insisted.

"Sure, heh, heh. Sorry about that kid," I thought to myself.

After they calmed Sammy down, we finally headed on up the trail. Sammy told me, "Dudley, I saw that ghost llama and it was dreadful looking, just like you said!"

I couldn't help it. I started to laugh at Sammy's very accurate description of himself.

"Stop making fun of me, Dudley! You're so mean!"

"O.K., Sorry Sammy. I guess I should tell you the truth. I kind of played a trick on you. You see, you didn't really see a ghost llama. You were actually just watching a television machine showing a program about llamas."

Then I patiently explained to Sammy about *Channel 34, W.A.M.A. LLAMA T.V.*, and about how you can stand in front of car or truck windows for hours and watch shows about white llamas all day long.

Needless to say, Sammy believed me, and now he thinks he's watching *W.A.M.A. LLAMA T.V.* whenever he sees his reflection in windows.

That Sammy takes the cake, doesn't he? But if Sammy *takes the cake*, our two little cats take the cake and *eat* it to boot! You'll see what I mean in the next chapter.

CHAPTER 6

THE CATS

L.T., Steamer, and Cud Face

According to often-told family stories, the two felines in our family came into the home as strays. They were all alone in the world, with no one to give them food or love.

The mom thinks that people are supposed to take in strays and adopt them whenever possible, and so when she's able to, she does. She even believes that God tries to match certain strays up with certain people, that it's all planned out ahead of time.

Now, I'm not sure that I believe all of this, but she says that when a person meets such a stray, they can feel it in their heart. Sammy and I weren't strays, but she also thinks that we were both meant to be part of her family, too. Who knows for certain? Maybe she's right.

In the case of the stray cat, L.T., the mom found her on a farm she was visiting with her little brown-but-now-green hat girl troop. I'll tell you about this zany troop in a later chapter.

Anyway, L.T. was a tiny, sick, starving, flea-bitten kitten, born to a mother stray that lived on the farm. The farm owner told the mom, "Oh, I just rounded up that litter of wild kittens yesterday and took them to the animal pound to be destroyed. I guess I missed that one somehow. I'll have to make another trip to the pound with that one later this week."

Well, the little girl troop overheard this conversation, and they all cried for the poor little, unloved kitten. Each of them called home to ask permission to bring the stray home, but all of the mothers said, "No way!"

The mom in our family cried about the kitten, too, and that's when she started to feel that special feeling in her heart that I told you about. So she took the little cat home and gave it lots of care and love and good food.

The mom named the kitten "Little Trooper" after the girl troop. The family calls her L.T. for short, or some-times just "T" for really short. But whenever she hisses at me, I call her "Missy Hissy Little Terrible." If she could spit at me then, she would, but cats can't spit. They can't pucker up their tiny mouths the way you have to, to spit. Unlike cats, we gifted llamas are *practically perfect prankish patooie pucksters.* I dare you to say that three times, really fast!

Well, it didn't take long before L.T. became

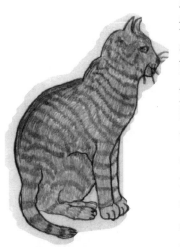 healthy, fat and annoying. And speaking of annoying, Steamer, the boy cat, was a stray the people mom found in Steamboat Springs and so they call him "Steamer," or sometimes just '*Boat* for short. Come to think of it, though, Steamer will answer to just about anything you'd care to call him. If you were to holler, "Come here you big goof," Steamer would come right away, meowing all the while as he jumps right into your arms. What a kissup!

As Annie Dog tells the story, the dad had never liked cats before the mom brought L.T. into the family, and he used to say, "Cats fly best when launched by tail!" Or, "I like cats. They taste like chicken." Pretty mean, huh? This is the same dad who tells the mom to stop treating Sammy and me so much like "pets" and more like "beasts of burden," remember?

But guess what? This same dad now carries these cats around and pets them and kisses them and lets them sleep on his bed. You see, cats have some magical charm they use on people, and the people fall for it every time. Even Annie thinks the two cats are "so cute."

To be honest with you, I agree that cats *LOOK* kind of cute with their delicate whiskers, little pointy ears and tiny noses. But their behavior is far from cute, in *my* humble opinion.

Our two cats are always getting into everything, knocking things over, getting stuck in tight places, sticking their tongues out, hissing at us, and fighting with each other.

Cats are so snoopy and curious that they always have to get right in the middle of *everything* anyone is working on in the barn. They try to

Typical nosey cat!

climb into any and all open boxes and containers and pry around in them, usually making terrible messes. They wreck rugs and sofas with their claws.

They get stuck up in trees and on top of roofs, and they get up onto counter tops and tables and steal people food, sometimes right off of plates or out of pots on the stove. Annie is my witness to all of this.

Steamer also leaves dead mice and birds in our barn stalls for us as "presents." Absolutely, positively, and totally gross! Llamas are vegetarians, and the only things we ever kill are pesky flies and mosquitoes in the summertime. We certainly never *EAT* them!

But do the cats ever get into trouble for any of this? Nooo--not on your life! Instead, the people, and even Annie, think cat behavior is "charming." Go figure!

When Annie notices the cats sleeping in the barn in funny places and positions, she says, "Look at those two, Dudley, asleep on that hay bale! Doesn't she look sweet all curled up like that? And look at Steamer, sleeping on his back. How adorable!"

And in this family, cats are allowed to cuddle in laps at any time, even immediately after being mischievous, no questions asked!

Annie tells us about how "funny" it is when Steamer chews up shoelaces and watchbands and glasses cases and eats anything made of leather.

Then he gets a tummy ache and has to go to the animal doctor. But do the people or Annie get upset with him for any of this? Nooo. Of course not! But when Yours Truly merely spits at Sammy, or stops for a just a second when we're hiking on a trail to grab a bite of grass, or to go to the bathroom while crossing a stream, then it's a totally different story. Then it's,

"No Dudley, stop eating the bark off the tree!"

"Bad llama, Dudley! You shouldn't eat the columbine flowers!"

"Stop spitting at your brother, Dudley!"

"No stopping now, Dudley!"

"No stopping *HERE,* Dudley!"

"Don't pee in the stream, Dudley. Keep moving!"

"No grazing while walking, Dudley! You know that!"

"Stop trying to go the wrong way, Dudley! Follow your leader!"

And "blah, blah, blah."

Now, L.T. is older and smarter than Steamer. She's great at being aloof and is very particular as to when and if she wants attention. Steamer, on the other hand, takes attention whenever and wherever it's offered. The children can even hold him upside down and tickle his belly, and he just purrs back at them.

So to the people, Steamer is like "Mr. Mellow." But every now and then, he turns into a mean, stalking jungle cat, stealthily tracking down his poor, unsuspecting victim, L.T.

Steamer, who is twice L.T.'s size, runs at her, knocks her over, bites, and uses his sharp claws on her. Fur flies, she screams bloody

murder, and the people come a'running. But does Steamer ever get punished for any of this violence, like I do when I merely *spit* at Sammy? Of course not! He just sits there looking totally innocent as L.T. runs away in a huff, angry at the world, even at the people who just rescued her from him.

"Why'd they have to bring *him* into this family? One cat's enough and I was here first! Take him back to the streets or I'm running away from home!," she pouts. Of course, she never runs away for very long. The mom always finds her and cuddles with her until she's calmed down.

L.T. eats only cat food, but Steamer also devours green vegetables like broccoli and brussels sprouts, as well as mice, birds, slugs, grasshoppers, spiders and crickets. L.T. looks at him scornfully when he feasts on such fare and she tells him, "You are *so* disgusting, Steamer! Simply disgusting!" Steamer just grins back at her and says, "Why thank you, L.T.. You know how very much I aim to please you!"

People always laugh at Sammy and me when we munch up mouthfuls of long grass, but at least the food we ingest doesn't try to hop, crawl, or fly away before we eat it!

These two felines are always getting into our pannier bags, the packs Sammy and I carry on our saddles, which hold the people stuff when we go camping. They make big messes of the bags, pulling things out and often trying to become stow-aways on our hikes.

Once one of them even used a pannier bag as a litter box, but I won't tell you which one. Now, I don't mean that I won't tell you which pannier bag--it was one of Sammy's, thank goodness--but that I won't snitch on which cat, although he's big and bulky and his first name starts with an "S." Need any more clues?

One day when Sammy and I were stretching our long necks over the pasture fence, trying to reach the new and tender-tasting aspen leaves--a real no-no with the mom--we heard a tremendous commotion down at the barn. It sounded much louder than the usual cat squabble, with ear-piercing screeches, hissing and caterwauling, all mixed together. Then we heard an incredibly loud *R O A R!!,* and we knew that some other very big animal was in the barn with the cats.

Being such curious creatures, we ran pell-mell to the barn for a look-see. When we arrived, we were shocked to discover a huge, and I mean *HUGE!,* cat, up on a wooden box, towering over our two little cats. He had cornered them down

below him in one of our empty pannier bags. He knocked the whole bag down onto the floor, cats and all!

"HOLY HUM HUM! HOLY CO W! ALARM!! ALARM!! THE CATS! OUR CATS! PROTECT OUR CATS!!"

Sammy's warning system went off immediately, just in time to startle the monstrous cat and distract him from swiping his gigantic clawed paw at our two tiny cats below him.

Sammy's instant maneuver bought me just enough time to bring up a great big wad of my green cud, the worst kind of smelly spit a llama can make, and *PA T O O IE! SPLA T!!* I hit him smack-dab in the middle of his face! That

stunned him for a second, and then the smell of cud finally reached his nose, and he leaped into the air in fright! When he fell back down, he hit part of the barn wall. *THUD!* " *A L L RIGHT, DUDSEY! GREAT SHOT!,*" Sammy shouted.

The big cat slowly picked himself up. He was looking a little dazed and standing a bit unsteadily on his feet, as he tried unsuccessfully to wipe off the foul-smelling cud with his large paw. He unwittingly made it worse by smearing it into his eyes.

Sammy and I raced back and forth, shrieking and jumping up and down ferociously, like two berserk llamas. For you see, as spoiled and as annoying as those two little cats can be, they are still *OUR* two little cats, and no two-hundred pound bully was going to hurt even a whisker on their cute little faces. Not if Sammy and I could help it!

Bellowing out an angry roar and threatening us with his sharp fangs, the unhappy Mr. Cud Face then looked at us puzzled and confused, as if to say, "*Whatever* is your *problem,* you two maniacs?"

Annie Dog arrived just in time to bark some German indignities at him, adding insult to injury, and so he turned quickly and sprinted away, thank goodness!

"Auf Wiedersehen du grosse scardy Katze!" Annie shouted after him, as usual mixing up her German and English. "Yes indeed, goodby you big scardy cat!" I repeated in llama hum.

I filled Annie in on all of the details, and then I told Sammy, "Well, bro, I guess the two things Cud Face understands best are Dead-Eye Dudley aims and German insults!" All three of us laughed long and hard.

"Ja, ja, llamas, da haben wir's!" added Annie, which in English means, "Yes, yes, llamas, that has done the trick!"

By the time the people showed up to investigate the commotion, the emergency was all over. Steamer and L.T. were already hiding up in the barn loft, and wonderfully, they stayed up there for the rest of the day, giving us some peace and quiet for once.

The dad discovered very large cat tracks in the dirt outside of the barn, and he said, "The tracks were made by a mountain lion."

"Oh, so that's what Cud Face is called," I told Sammy, 'a mountain lion!' Well, now he's a mountain lion with green smelly goop on his face!"

The mom told the dad, "The mountain lion must have been scared away by the way the llamas look and smell. Thank goodness neither of them was hurt!"

"Hey, wait just a minute," I hummed. "What does she mean by the way we "look and smell?" That doesn't sound like a compliment to me, does it to you Sammy? Too bad she doesn't understand how we three brave-hearted musketeers saved her two precious little felines for her! HA! What an ingrate!"

But, just as soon as I got done humming out that complaint to Sammy, the mom looked at us and said, "Thanks, guys, for making the mountain lion feel unwelcome. We really appreciate all the protection you give us around here. You're very brave llamas."

"Whoa!" I thought. "The mom's a mind reader. Spooky!"

* * * * * *

Later, after things had calmed down a little, Sammy asked me to teach him how to spit cud. First, I explained to him that cud is a llama's *secret weapon*, to be used *only* on our worst enemies. After he agreed to that, I explained that cud was just green smelly regurgitated grass which we can bring up from the first of our three stomach chambers, to spit when we're greatly angry or afraid. It's totally vile, fermented stuff--perfect ammo for defense purposes. Cattle and sheep chew cud, but they can't spit it, poor things.

"Regurgitate" is a neat-sounding word, isn't it, and it just means to bring something very

smelly up from your stomach, so you'll probably
want to add it to your collection of gross
vocabulary words.

Anyway, I showed Sammy exactly how to
do it, but I said he should save his first try for the
next time Steamer picks on L.T. Sammy decided
that was a pretty good idea, that "Steamer would
certainly have it coming! I hope my aim is good."

Sammy got his chance on the very next
day. When we noticed Steamer beginning to
stalk L.T., following her quietly into the barn,
Sammy and I tiptoed behind him, and we both
gave Steamer "a taste of his own medicine," as the
dad likes to call it. Since then, Steamer hasn't
even once attacked L.T., at least not when he's
been in the barn area within our firing range.
And come to think of it, L.T. *does* seem to have a

much better disposition these days. Perhaps it's due to the behavior modification technique which we now use on the 'Boat Boy!

Meanwhile, Sammy and I picked out a certain post in the fence to practice on, and now it looks totally disgusting. The dad can't figure out what's making such a big, smelly green mess on that particular post, but Sammy and I know.

"Yahoo! *P A T O O I E !!*

Sammy can't wait to try out his new talent on an elk or on another mountain lion, should one be stupid enough to venture into our llama domain again!

"Now that winter is just about here, Sammy, perhaps you'll only get to target practice on unsuspecting snowsnakes for a while."

"SNOWSNAKES?   DUDLEY, DID YOU SAY SNOWSNAKES?   WHERE ARE THEY?," Sammy hummed, in an agitated, nervous state of panic.

And speaking of snowsnakes, that reminds me of yet another fun time to tell you about in the next chapter. It sort of involves snowsnakes and old nurses and noisy little kids and old people and snowstorms and white hair. But let me explain.

CHAPTER 7

SNOWSNAKES AND

THE TRIP TO TOWN

One winter morning, when the sun was shining brightly off of the white snow in our pasture, Sammy and I were saddled and loaded into the trailer. Now, this was unusual because in the winter, we normally never get to go anywhere in the trailer. It aroused our curiosity greatly, to say the least.

"Dudley, where do you think they're taking us this time of year? It's winter, and there's far too much snow on the trails now to go hiking."

"Well, don't quote me on this, bro, but I think it has something to do with using llamas to clear snowsnakes off of the ski mountain in town. I heard Christopher say that there's quite an infestation of those white-fanged slimy slitherooes in the moguls."

I had totally made that up right there on the spot, but as usual, old gullible Sammy believed it and started to hum his Nervous Norvis hum, "Snowsnakes...snowsnakes...why would they think I'd be any good around snowsnakes? I don't even like to walk in snow, much less kill off snowsnakes in it! Oh hum, Oh dear..."

After riding for about half an hour, I guessed that we were in downtown Steamboat Springs. I could smell the stinky cars, and our trailer kept stopping and going, like it does when we go through a town.

"Where *are* we going, really?," I wondered. I hoped that they might be taking us to the ski mountain in town. I had never seen it myself, but Annie Dog had told me all about how the people

ride up in little cars hanging from a wire. They call the little cars "gone-to Dola's," so I think that somebody named Dola must live up at the top. After they get to Dola's place, they then slide down the steep hills at a gazillion miles an hour on the ski boards.

Annie said that she once went with the people to the bottom of the mountain where she and Claire and the big people watched Sarah and Christopher ride up in a little gone-to-Dola car. After about a half-hour wait, they watched as

Christopher!

the two children slid down to them from way atop the mountain on these funny ski boards. She said it looked like a lot of fun to her, but she couldn't join them because they don't let dogs ride on the gone-to-Dola cars. Big bummer!

I knew all about cross-country skiing because that's what my family does when I pull the sled on Seedhouse Road in the winter. I had never seen this down-the-hill skiing before and so I was looking forward to it, if, indeed, that's where they were taking us.

And as for snowsnakes, bring 'em on, the more the merrier! I've no fear!

As luck would have it, though, the ski mountain wasn't our destination, but we went instead to a building where they took little Claire a couple of mornings a week called a "nursing school." That's a funny name, but Annie and I figure they must teach little kids how to be nurses there or something.

When we entered the building, a whole herd of hopping, jumping, squealing small people flocked around me and Sammy. And what a terrible racket they made!

Yikes! "These children put my nerves on edge," as the mom often says about our own children at home.

The dad put panniers on our saddles, and then the kids took turns getting put into the panniers, one on each side for balance. They all thought it was great fun. ("Oh sure! For *them* maybe!")

The dad combed out a bunch of our wool and gave each child a little bit of it. Since it was winter, Sammy and I had thick coats, so losing a little like that didn't bother me. But I wasn't too crazy about all of the sticky fingers being rubbed on my neck, and I hummed a complaining hum. The dad told them about how llamas hum, but he got it all mixed up as usual and told them that I was humming a happy hum, "probably because Dudley is so happy to be with all of you today." (Wrong!)

One of these noisy munchkins reached up from the pannier bag and pulled on my ears, and then tried to poke out my eye! Well, I didn't like it one bit! I wanted to turn my head around and give him a good patooie spit, but I didn't dare because the spitting-back dad was right by my side.

Some llamas are being used these days for therapy for people who need calming and gentleness, but Sammy and I certainly didn't have that effect on this batch of boisterous bibble-babblers!

When the teacher lady told the dad that they had been studying Native American Indians and that "some of the children want to dress the llamas up with feathers and do a traditional Indian dance around them," the dad answered, "Certainly. Dudley and Sammy would love it, I'm sure."

"*YIKES!! HELP!!!*"I hummed out! "Get me *OUT* of here!!"

Sammy, of course, *did* love every minute of the feathers and the dance and the noise, and being with these rambunctious little moppets. He was also especially relieved to discover that there were absolutely *no* snowsnakes living at this nursing school. I told Sam the children had probably scared them all far away for good!

After awhile, the kids all said goodby to us, hugged us some more (yuck!), and then we were loaded into the trailer once again. "Ah, home sweet *quiet* home," I thought.

Instead of going home, though, we were taken to yet another parking area and then inside another building. But this place was much quieter than the kid place, thank my big lucky banana ears, which were still ringing from the last place.

We were led into a room full of very old, kindly-looking, white-haired people. Many of them were sitting in chairs that had wheels on them because their legs don't work too well anymore.

The mom told us we were in a "nursing home," so I figured that it must be a home for old people who used to be nurses.

"Hmmm," I hummed. "First a school for future nurses and then a home for retired nurses. I wonder why the dad's on this big nurse kick?," I asked Sam." "Beats me, Dudley, but nurses sure are fun!"

Everyone in the home was very sweet and gentle to us, and unlike the noisy kid place, I could have stayed with these sweet, calm, old people all day long.

They smiled at us and paid us many compliments, telling us that we're "handsome animals," and "so alert," and "very intelligent looking!"

Yes, indeed. Old white-haired people are *extremely* wise.

I, willingly, was on my very best behavior here. So was Sammy, but that was nothing new for him. And being white-haired himself, he felt right at home with these people.

After about an hour we said our goodbyes, and were then taken back outside. The weather had turned very snowy and the temperature was dropping very quickly. Sammy couldn't wait to get into the trailer.

"Hum, hum, hurry. Hum, hum, hurry. It's cold out here! Brrrrrr! Open the trailer, fast. Put us in, quickly! My feet are getting wet and cold! Brrrrr....hum, hum, hum."

The return trip home seemed to take forever. Looking out the air vents, I could see that snow was falling heavily. Sammy and I prayed that our trailer wouldn't slide off the road into a snowdrift, but our truck has four-wheel drive, just like us llamas, and it got us safely through the blizzard.

We huddled closely together to keep warm, and we both agreed that it would be wonderful to finally get home to our nice, snug barn and some water and hay.

By the time we arrived at our home sweet home, it was very dark out and still snowing like the chickens. I could barely see the mom out in front of me, trying to lead us to the barn. There was so much snow that the dad went ahead of us, shoveling out a bit of a path for us to follow. Sammy sort of blended in with the snow, and even though his lead was tied onto my saddle horns, I couldn't even see him behind me. For sure, I could hear his loud complaining hum somewhere back there, so I knew my bro was still safe.

We finally made it into the quiet barn, and I was greatly relieved. "Ah yes, home is where the *hay* is," I joked to Sam.

The dad gave us hay and some oats for a treat and said, "Good work today, you guys. Everyone certainly enjoyed you two! Goodnight now. See you boys in the morning. Sleep tight and don't let the bed bugs bite!"

"Bed bugs? Dudley, what are bed bugs?," Sammy asked. "Relax Sammy! Just think about it. Llamas don't sleep in beds, right? So why should we worry about bed bugs? Although I did see a gigantic, deadly, hairy tarantula spider in your stall yesterday afternoon. Well, goodnight bro."

All in all, it was a pretty strange, yet interesting sort of day. First we got to be around some little sticky-fingered, noisy, wiggly humans at a nursing school, and then around some very old, gentle, sweet, wise and quiet people at a home for old nurses. I guess humans start out all noisy and obnoxious like the little kids and end up nice and quiet like the old people. I wonder how many years it takes them in between to figure out how to end up that way? Too long, I'm afraid!

A little later on, after I nodded off to sleep, I dreamed that there was a pasture full of kind old llamas somewhere, wise elderly white-haired llamas, sitting around in chairs with wheels on them. And they all said, "Welcome home, Dudley. You're going to love it here." I looked down at the hair on my chest, and it was completely white.

I liked those old llamas a lot, so I kept my dream going for a long time and had a wonderful night in that pasture visiting with them. When I awoke the next morning I remembered my dream, and I wondered if there really was such a pasture somewhere?

Nah, probably not, but you never know!

Sammy, by the way, said he'd had "a very restless night." Seems the poor guy spent the night worrying about spiders and was now totally exhausted. I told him he could take a nap after breakfast, and that I would stay near and guard him from any poisonous tarantula spiders.

"Thanks, Dudley. Sometimes you're really a great brother, you know that?"

"Oh well. You know me. I do what I can, Sam, I do what I can."

After making that fun trip into town, we had to spend the rest of the winter stuck in our snow-filled pasture, and time sort of dragged by very slowly. Eventually, another summer did arrive, and we were more than ready for hiking and further adventures. Little did we know that a dangerous black creature would be part of one of those adventures.

No, it wasn't a tarantula spider. They don't live up at our altitude, by the way, but don't tell Sammy that.

So, as they say on *W.A.M.A. LLAMA T.V.*, "Stay tuned for more *llively llama* adventures!"

CHAPTER 8

BIG, BAD BEAST IN
THE NIGHT

During the third summer with my people family, in early July, Sammy and I were driven to a trailhead where our panniers were loaded up for a camping trip with the heavy things, like tents, sleeping bags, pots and pans, people food, and so on.

Except for our tether ropes and a little bit of oats, we llamas don't need to carry anything for ourselves. In the summer we can sleep out under the stars in any kind of weather, and we eat the grasses and leaves we find along the trail.

The mom likes to tell people, "Llamas are self-contained, just like Arvees." I'm not sure what kind of animals Arvees are, but the mom says they eat gasoline, so they must be stinky like cars.

"Incidently, we carry the oats along to be used as little treats or as *a bribe* for Dudley when he acts up and won't do what we tell him to," she says. It usually works since I love oats, almost as much as rocky trail ice cream cones and figgy newtons.

The people carried light day packs with their rain gear, cameras, jackets, toothbrushes and other small people things.

Now, those *toothbrushes* are of real interest to me, since I would very much like to have a good tooth brushing from time to time. Llamas have large teeth, but in Sammy's and my case, only on the bottom. Our owners very wisely removed our two top sharp fighting teeth so that we won't hurt each other when we fight or bite, making us toothless on top. So I'd like to take better care of the teeth I do have left with daily tooth brushings, preferably using wildflower-extract or rocky trail ice cream-flavored toothpaste. *Yum!*

Annie Dog told me about a song she heard a little girl sing on the Sesame Seed show once, about taking her llama to the dentist to have its teeth cleaned. What a llucky llama!

But now back to the camping trip story. Where was I? Oh yes, now I remember.

We were hiking up the North Fork of the Elk River. Fortunately, this isn't a very steep trail since it was still early summer and Sammy wasn't yet in good pack-animal shape. He hummed his moaning and groaning hum, complaining about having to carry "far too much weight," so I was happy that we weren't going up to Mica Lake or to North Lake, two much harder climbs.

As for me, I'm tough and always in pretty good shape because in the winter, I patrol the pasture and pull the sled on the road. But as I told you, Sammy doesn't like to walk in deep snow, and so he doesn't get much exercise during the winter months. Usually, he hangs out in the barn until late morning when the sun warms things up. Then, if it's not snowing, he ventures out into the snow-packed pasture for awhile and soaks in some of the sun's rays. But at sundown, or if the white flakes begin to come down, *ZIP!*, he's right back in the warm barn eating the hay. Now, *that's* what I call a "fair weather llama!"

Personally, I almost always prefer to be outside, unless there's a terrible storm raging. During very cold, snowy weather, I try to hang out in the barn, especially at night. For you see, I hate to fall asleep outside in the pasture and wake up covered with about four feet of snow. Two of

the children saw me like this one morning, and they thought I was a big snow-covered haystack. When I popped my head up through the snow at them, they laughed so hard! Now during snowstorms, those smarty-pants kids tease me, "Dudley, stay outside tonight and you'll get to be the Abominable Snowman again in the morning." "Go ahead, make fun of me, you awful kidlets!," I hum at them.

During the first few weeks of summer, Sammy has to hike himself into shape, and he grumbles about it the whole time. Me, I can carry up to a hundred and twenty pounds with no problems, but Sammy doesn't like to carry more than fifty pounds. When he has to, he hums his griping hum along most of the trail. The people don't know that this is a complaining hum, since, generally speaking, only other llamas know for *certain* what our various hums mean. People often try to guess, but as I told you before, they usually guess wrong.

For example, most of the time people think that our happy hums mean we're worried and our worried hums mean we're happy, and so on. You get the idea. I, on the other hand, *know* that Sammy is humming his complaining hum, and quite frankly, after a couple of hours it begins to jangle my nerves.

"Put a cork in it, Sammy!," I tell him, or "Will you put a lid on it, bro?" But to no avail.

If no people are watching, I'll put my ears

113

back on my head, lift my head way back, gurgle up some spit, and then *PATOOIE!*, I'll quickly give Sammy a good spray of llama saliva. It's not nearly as bad as cud, but it's usually enough to shut him up for about ten minutes or so, and then he's back to hum, hum, bellyaching.

We llamas are two-toed animals, with soft pads on the bottoms of our feet. Just like deer, we usually hike very quietly up a trail--except for Sammy's complaining humming, that is.

Sometimes when people think Sammy is humming a happy hum instead of the fussing hum which he is actually humming, they hum back at him, and right in his face, too. Then they kiss him and hug him, and nuzzle noses, and Sammy not only puts up with it all, but he actually enjoys it. Poor guy doesn't seem to know any better!

Not me though. I don't like kisses of any sort, wet ones *or* dry ones. And I don't like people to touch my face. Now, sometimes I'll rest my head on top of a human's head or on their shoulder, if my neck is tired--"Awww, Dudley's so sweet!" Or, I might just blow softy into a person's face or on the back of their neck if I like them a lot, but that's as close as I like to get to showing affection. After all, I'm a *boy* llama, not a *mama* llama. The people just eat that sort of affection stuff up, though.

I don't mind it if people I'm fond of blow softly back into my face, as long as they haven't
114

been eating raw onions or garlic that day. *That* could kill a llama straight-out! Because of our diet of grass, our breaths are almost always sweet as newly-mowed hay.

Annie Dog, unlike Yours Truly, is always very af-fectionate. She gives slurpy wet dog kisses to the people all of the time, and watching her do that sort of upsets my stomach. But as the people like to say, "different folks for different strokes."

Now where was I? Oh, yes. Sorry about that. I keep trying to tell you about the camping trip we were on, up the North Fork trail, but I guess my story keeps hiking off the trail!

Anyway, after about a four mile hike, we finally stopped and set up a nice camp a bit over one hundred feet away from the river. You're supposed to camp at least that far away from all water sources so that you don't pollute them.

Sammy and I watched the mom and dad put two tents up, collect firewood, and filter water into containers for drinking. People say there are tiny bugs in the water that might make them sick, so they pour the water through a filter that traps

115

the bugs.

When they let us, Sammy and I can drink right out of streams and rivers, and it doesn't bother us at all. The water always looks so clean that I can see the trout fish, but never any tiny bugs. But Sammy and I know enough not to suck up any trout fish when we drink.

And speaking of trout fish, while the mom and dad were busy setting up the campsite, the children ran to the river with long stick-like poles. The poles seemed to have some sort of magic string attached to the ends because, whenever they threw the string out into the water, they would soon pull up a wiggly fish.

Trout!

Something made the string stick to the fish or the fish to the string, whichever. Maybe it was magic fish glue?

Later, the mom cooked the trout fish over the campfire, and they ate green beans, baked potatoes and baked apples for dinner, along with the fish. For our dinner, Sammy and I ate willow bushes with fireweed wildflowers for dessert. Yum, yum.

I for one would never eat anything which once wiggled or had eyes or a heartbeat, but I'll bet you Sammy would eat a fish if they told him

116

to. He'd probably even eat a snake, although not a snowsnake since he's afraid of them, and also since they don't really exist.

Later on that night, the people sat around their campfire for a long time. The mom kept telling the children, "Please stop putting more wood on the fire! It's high enough!" She always tells them that, yet they keep sneaking more wood onto the fire. It's just a kid kind of thing to do, I guess. Plus, I think the mom telling them that is more of the "it goes in one ear and out the other" communication problem that she has with them. She often tells the dad, "When I talk to the children, I might just as well be talking to a wall!" Now, I don't understand why anyone would want to talk to a wall, but then there's a lot of things I don't understand about humans.

The mom played her noisy guitar thing, and the rest of the family howled along with her. They call it "singing songs," and they like to howl about animals and nature and goofy stuff. Some of it is pretty silly, like the one about a man by the name of "Old McDonald." The children make all sorts of animal noises during the song, but I think they're best at the pig noises, "Oink, oink, here, an oink, oink, there, here an oink, there an oink, everywhere an oink, oink..."

Humans truly amaze me!

After the howling session was over, the children held sticks with white globs stuck on the ends over the fire. The white globs soon started on fire and turned into melted black globs. Then they put these hot, badly-burned black blobs into their mouths and actually *ate* them! Can you

118

believe it? And people laugh at Sammy and me when we gobble down pine needles and bark. As Chris always says, "Go figure!"

Then the dad called everybody together just before bedtime and told them he wanted ALL of the food in camp to be put into a big bag which he held.

"Don't forget anything," he told them, "and especially don't keep any food inside of your tent. That's really important."

He took the big bag to a large dead tree a little bit behind where Sammy and I were tethered. He threw a long rope over a high branch of the tree, and then he tied the end of the rope onto the bag and pulled it up. Next, he tied the other end of the rope to another branch, and he left the bag dangling down from the high branch.

"Why would anybody want to hang food up in a tree like that?" I asked Sammy.

"You got me, Dudley. Maybe he's afraid Christopher will get up in the night and eat it all up. You know how much that boy likes to eat!"

"Well, they certainly aren't trying to protect their food from *us*, bro, unless there's some rocky trail inside of that bag."

"Hey, wait a minute, Sam, do you think they're going to play that mean game again, the one they played at Sarah's last birthday party, remember? They hung that poor paper donkey up on the rafter in our barn and tied something around the kids' eyes and let them whack at the poor thing with a bat until they smashed it open!"

"Oh, yeah, I remember that! And then candy fell out of it and all the children scrambled around on the ground, acting and sounding like pigs at a trough--oink, oink, oink. Gimme', gimme', gimme'! Sure, I bet you're right, Duds, that's probably what they're going to do again in the morning. Maybe it's somebody's birthday tomorrow?"

But Sammy and I were soon to learn the *real* reason for the strange custom of hanging food up in a tree when camping.

They tethered Sammy and me to the ground on long ropes so that we could graze or sleep all night long without wandering away. Little do they know that, after our encounter with the snotty elk and the hunters that time, they didn't have to worry about Sammy or me taking off on them ever again.

I soon ate my full of the camp grasses, folded my legs under me, and laid down. I could hear the river running nearby, and it was a very loud but restful sound. I soon fell fast asleep.

A couple hours later, though, my nose woke me up. *Sniff, sniff,* it smelled a disgusting, pungent odor, and in spite of the loud river noise, my alert ears heard a snorting sound coming from the area of the children's tent.

Now, I know that children often have a stinky odor about them and that kids also make pig noises a lot, like when they eat their lunches or howl the Old McDonald song or play the mean hit-the-donkey game, but *this* smell and noise was far worse than what the children ever made! "Kids smell sweet next to this smell," I thought.

I quickly dragged my tether rope over as closely to the children's tent as I could get it, and

immediately, my llama alarm went off.

"ALARM!! ALARM!!" I wailed! *"WHAT ARE YOU? GET AWAY FROM MY CHILDREN! DON'T YOU HURT MY CHILDREN! GET AWAY FROM THEM!!"* In a hot flash, the German K-9 was by my side, and together we fiercely barked

121

and whined at this monster which now turned and faced us. I spit my cud at it, but this creature was so furry and stinky itself that the smelly cud didn't even phase it.

Thankfully, it backed away from our children's tent--startled, no doubt, by our display of bravery and frightful noises!

The dad appeared, shining a flashlight on the furry blob, and we could see its white, nasty-looking fangs. Unlike Sammy and me, these creatures have teeth on the tops *and* the bottoms, and they're sharp pointy teeth to boot. *YIKES!*

The dad clapped his hands together at the blob, and Annie and I added our two-cents' worth of threatening snarls and llama whines. The uproar was probably enough to wake the dead, but unfortunately, this nasty guy was very much the opposite of dead!

It suddenly stood up on its hind legs, and brother, was it *BIG!* Then it waddled right at me, letting out a fierce, threatening *ROAR!*

"*OOOPS,*" I thought. I'm like a big dope on a rope on this tether line. I can't run away from this brute. I'm in deep trouble now!"

Sensing my predicament, instead of running away herself, Annie Dog lunged at the big creature, hit it and bounced off it. This dog maneuver made the creature turn its attention away from me and toward Annie Dog.

The blob swiped at Annie and drew blood. She yelped in pain but bravely stood her ground, snarling and barking her deepest, fiercest, loudest bark. I started to rise up and kick at the creature with my sharp front toes. Its claws got me a good one on my left front leg, and that really, *really* hurt and made me even more angry! Then I had a total fit. If this monster was going to try to hurt our children or kill my Annie Dog, it was going to have to kill *me* first. I wasn't going down without first putting up a dilly of a fight!

BANG!! BANG!! BANG!!

An absolutely ear-splitting noise shocked Annie and me as much as it did the angry blob. As the mom shined a flashlight on it, the dad banged two pots together, hard and furious, and he shouted at the top of his lungs, *"GET OUT OF HERE!! LEAVE OUR PETS ALONE, YOU NASTY BEAR!"*

To add to the confusion, all three children were, by now, screaming in the dark tent. At this terrible brouhaha, the big fur ball took one look at the angry man and woman, the berserk llama and the infuriated, crazed German Shepherd, and thank our lucky stars, it backed away from us until it finally just turned and began to leave. As it did so, it picked up a plastic bag next to the tent, and it dragged it along on the ground, spilling out round chocolate candies as it retreated.

We were all so relieved!

We were all so alive!

The dad gathered everyone around a lantern and told us the invader had been a huge

123

black bear which had ripped a hole in the children's tent to get at a bag of candy hidden inside by some "disobedient child."

Just which child it was, I'm not at liberty to say, but the dad then gave them all a lecture about "caching" food away from bears, telling them in a gruff voice, "Let this be a good lesson to you. Don't ever keep any food in your tent in bear country, unless you want to share your tent and your food with a bear. You have to hang it all high up on a tree branch, away from your camp, just like I did last night. Then the bears can't get at it and will leave you and your camp alone!"

The dad then told the guilty child that he or she was "grounded from candy for two months!" I think that meant that they had to eat candy off of the ground for two months, but I'm not completely sure about this. I never actually *saw* this guilty child eating candy off of the ground, but perhaps I just missed it.

The mom, meanwhile, hugged Annie and told her once again how smart and brave and wonderful she was. I, for one, knew this to be the absolute and honest-to-goodness truth.

Then the mom also hugged me and told me how brave I had been. Now, I have to admit that I actually kind of enjoyed this hug, for the very first time in my whole life! Wow! What's happening to me, I wondered?

The dad put some stinging medicine on Annie and my cuts and said, "Don't worry, Sarah, the cuts don't look very bad. I think these two must have had some angels looking out for them!"

I hadn't seen any angels looking out for us, but then again, I don't know what angels look like.

Luckily, the mom didn't try to kiss *me*, like she did to Annie on her nose. Yuck! That would have been too much, too soon, for me.

When I looked at Annie, I suddenly felt a warm feeling inside of me, just about where I think my heart probably is. Without thinking about what I was doing, I walked over to her and said, "Thank you for risking your life for me, Annie Dog. That smelly bear was about *ten times your size*! I love you." As I said this, tears welled up in my eyes, and a couple actually spilled out.

Annie Dog looked a little surprised, and

125

perhaps even a little embarrassed. But then she replied, "Well, Dudley, I've always known that you love me. Now you just know that I love you back, O.K.?"

Meanwhile, Sammy came trudging over to us, looking very confused and concerned. Amazingly, he had slept through all of the

commotion. He said that he had heard something awful, but that he had thought it was all part of a bad dream he was having. He just kept sleeping to find out if the dream turned out all right, but the pots and pans finally woke him up for real, and now he wanted to know what the ruckus had all been about.

"Well, sleeping beauty," I told him, "a huge black bear came into our camp, so big he could reach the food bag way up in the tree. He ate up all of the people food, and then Annie and I chased him off. But now the people will have to eat llama meat, so we volunteered *you*, Sammy."

The look on his face was classic, kind of like the same look a llama gets when it eats a big mouthful of thistle plant by mistake!

CHAPTER 9

THE REUNION

I could smell it as soon as we arrived, the familiar odor of my babyhood home, the Rainbow Mountain Llama Ranch. Almost fifty llamas live on that ranch, and so the air smelled *tremendously invigorating* to me!

It was mid-summer of the same year as our bear encounter, and Sammy and I were loaded into the trailer and pulled along for a very brief time. When we arrived, sweet memories came flooding back into my head as I stepped out of the trailer and shouted, "*Wow!* I remember this place, Sammy! This is where I was born, and this is where my mama still lives, I hope!"

My pretty mama

Looking around a little, I quickly spotted her, my mama llama-- my oh-so-pretty mama llama! "Look, Sammy! There she is!"

128

She was just where I had left her, in the big pasture with the other mamas and babies, all now new to me.

I hummed my greeting hum to her, but she didn't hear me. "Mama llama! Morningstar! Look over here! It's me, your Dudley!"

I couldn't run over to her pasture because my lead was tied to a post. So I hummed out a few louder, and yet-*louder* greetings, and Morningstar *finally* looked up in my direction. Then she hurried over to the fence, getting as close to us as possible.

"Oh Dudley! Is that really *YOU* sweetheart? Why, it is! What a wonderful surprise!! What are you doing here? Have they sent you back? Did you misbehave too much? Oh dear! How have you been? We've all missed you! And just look at how you've grown into such a handsome, strong fellow!"

At that, I blushed, even though I knew she spoke the complete, honest truth.

"Hi mama!! Yes, it's me, your Dudley. How are you? How have you been? No, I don't think I've been sent back for misbehaving. I'm not any worse than when I left here!"

We hollered out our conversation, back and forth, and my heart felt great happiness! Although I couldn't get very close to her, I could see her beautiful big doe eyes with those pretty, curly, long lashes, and I knew that those eyes were still filled with love for me. My heart felt all

129

warm and jiggly inside, like it had the time I told Annie that I loved her. Sammy said it made him really happy to see me so happy. "Thanks, Sam. I hope I get to meet your mama some day, too."

Then, as if that wasn't enough joy for one day, four other boy llamas were brought in from the far pasture, and I knew all four of them! Two were Hansey and Zirkel, my cousins, and one was Lucky, my little brother. We had all been terribly-behaved baby boy llamas together, and we were now so delighted to see each other!

The fourth llama was Old Phil. He was pretty easy to recognize because his neck doesn't work right, and he sort of sticks it out in front of him instead of straight up like llamas usually do. And because he can't bend his neck down, he has to kneel down on his front knees just to eat and

Sammy and Old Phil
in lupine flowers

drink, and he always looks very odd, sort of like he's praying.

When I was little and still lived at the ranch, a lot of the boy llamas used to make fun of Old Phil and laugh and spit at him. I hate to admit it, but I did too. But then my mama llama once saw me doing it, and she took me aside and *read me the riot act*! She told me she was very disappointed in me, that I had really let her down.

Morningstar also said that Phil couldn't help his neck being that way, that he'd been born like that, and it was so cruel to make fun of him. Phil, she said, was a kind, gentle, loyal llama, and he always worked as hard as he could and never complained about anything.

"He's one of the few male llamas around here, Dudley, who doesn't have an ego problem. He has a wonderful sense of humor and never spits back or feels sorry for himself, either. He just does his job and makes the best of things and is always very respectful and polite to all of us mama llamas. You boys could all learn some lessons from Old Phil. Perhaps if you try to spend some time around him, if you're lucky, some of his goodness will rub off on you!"

I never got to do that, though, since I was taken away from the ranch soon after she gave me that advice.

In my heart, I now felt so ashamed that I had ever laughed at and spat at Old Phil, and I vowed to make it up to him somehow. Annie

131

Dog, who is so wise, as you now know, taught me that you should never judge a book by its cover. In other words, never judge somebody by just the way they look on the outside, by the color of their skin or fur, or by parts of their body which might not look perfect or work perfectly well. Annie says we should try to look at others more with our hearts than with our eyes.

It seems to me that often the people or animals which aren't so pretty or perfect on the outside have the most beautiful insides, and what's inside is far more important than what's on the outside. I finally had learned all of that.

Somehow I knew right away that Sammy would hit it off with Old Phil. Both of them are sort of like two *pods in a pea*--or is it *peas in a pod?* Whatever.

Sammy's neck isn't deformed, but he and Phil have such similar personalities, and they're both all white in color. It wouldn't surprise me if Old Phil isn't related to Sammy somehow, like maybe an uncle or even grandfather. They certainly act like they came from the same pod, and probably from outer space, too, since they're both so nice.

Delighted to be together again, we hummed and nuzzled at each other's ears. Llamas like to do that when we get angry or excited. When we're irked at each other, we try to bite the ears hard, but when we're happy to see one another, we sort of fake bite. As long as we're

132

with llamas whose top teeth have been removed, our bites can't do too much damage.

I'm sure this activity sounds strange to you, but believe me, we llamas think it's much fun! And speaking of ears and fun, just in case you haven't noticed in our pictures, we llamas often use our ear positions to express our moods. We can make them go every which way, something most humans can't do at all, at least none that I've ever seen.

I introduced my relatives to Sammy, who was more than a little bit worried to be around this many new male llamas. I told him not to fret, that these guys were much nicer than me, and this seemed to reassure him. I made my relations promise *NOT* to spit at Sammy or Phil, no matter what, and they were especially nice to them the whole time we were together.

Soon, all six of us were loaded into a very big trailer and off we went, riding for about an hour-and-a-half. I had plenty of time to catch up on all that had happened at the ranch since I'd left.

They filled me in on all of the new babies which had been born and about the fights in the pasture among the males to see who the *boss llama* would be.

They shared as much of the mama llama gossip as they knew, told to them by the young males who come to join them when they get to be about a year to a year-and-a-half old. Then I went

133

on and on to them about our Annie Dog and our pesky cats and our kids and the big people and our property, and also about the mountain lion and the smelly bear. Sammy sometimes rolled his eyes as he listened to me, for you see, he thinks I tend to exaggerate at times. I wonder where he got that idea?

We were going on an overnight camping trip with the McDuffy family, the people who own the Rainbow Mountain Llama Ranch. They are friends with my own people, and this is why they were teaming us up with some of their llamas, just for old Tymes' sake, they said, whoever *he* is!

After they loaded up our panniers with all of the supplies, we hiked down a beautiful, long trail which follows along pretty Sarvis Creek.

"These trees and grasses and rocks and the creek are some of the most see Nic around," the mom said. I searched with my eyes, but I didn't see any Nick guy around, and I wondered who

The hike up Sarvis Creek Trail

she was talking about?

I did get to visit with each of my relatives one by one, though, when the people leading us switched around in different orders on the trail as the day wore on. Of course, as we hiked along like that, I was basically either talking to a cousin's behind or a cousin was talking to my behind, but it was still a memorable visit.

Just as I had suspected, Sammy and Phil instantly became good friends, and Sammy insisted on always being put next to Phil in line. Usually, Sammy never insists on anything, so the people noticed this right away and gave him his way.

I had never seen Sammy so happy, and he didn't hum even one complaining hum on the whole trip, although he carried almost a hundred pounds. I guess he had finally found his soul mate, another llama who understood and appreciated him just the way he is.

That night, the people staked us out all together on our tether lines in a pretty meadow, lush with wildflowers and different-tasting grasses. We had such a pleasant time munching and visiting all night long--*yack, yack, yamma yakking.* I got little sleep, so packing out the next day was very tiring.

By the time we made it back to our trailer, I was *totally* exhausted, but incredibly happy! I guess this just proves the fact that llamas are highly sociable animals. I'm glad I wasn't born a *lone wolf.*

We returned to the ranch, and just before the dad switched Sam and me into our little trailer, I was able to hum out, "Goodby mama! Goodby Morningstar! I Love you! Oh, by the way, this is Sammy! He's my brother! Isn't he *great?*"

"Hi Sammy! Nice to meet you! I'm so happy Dudley has a nice brother llama to live with! Keep him out of trouble for me, will you?"

Sammy laughed and then said to me, "Good luck with *that* task, huh Dudley?"

My mama blew a goodby kiss to each of us, and they landed right on our big noses--*smack!* The kiss gave me that warm feeling inside my llama heart again.

Old Phil had promised to fill my mama in on all the things I had told him about on our trip, and that made me very happy.

That night, back in our own pasture, I thought about how all the llamas at the ranch get to be around so many other llamas, but all Sammy and I have at our place, as far as llamas go, is each other. It made me realize how grateful I am to have my brother, Sammy. I might not be related to him by blood, but you know, I feel like I am. I wanted to tell him that I loved him, but I just couldn't make the words come out of my mouth. So I just told him, "Sammy, did I ever tell

you I'm glad that you're my brother?" Sammy
smiled and said, "Really, Dudley? Wow!
Thanks. Me too!"

CHAPTER 10

THE MIXED MOUNTAIN CHORUS

Do you like to sing around a campfire? My family surely does, and so does the giggly gang of green-hat girls that Sarah hangs out with.

In August of that year, Sammy and I were surrounded at a trailhead by Sarah and a flock of these noisy little fillies. They all were dressed in green hats and scarves, and they put a scarf on my neck and Annie's and Sammy's, too. How embarrassing! One of them carried a little green flag with the number 429 on it. I guess that's how many they've learned how to count up to or something.

The day before, Sammy and I had packed in a bunch of supplies to a campsite, and now the little girls were going to hike to that camp to spend the night. On this second trip in, Sammy and I carried the rest of the camping gear and the fresh food.

The girls all wore small packs, but they mostly just carried light things like peanut butter and jelly sandwiches and teddy bears which poked their heads up out of the packs. As I walked behind these teddy bears, I kept nibbling on their cute little ears--very gently, of course. The girls never noticed. Not until later that evening, that is.

"OH GROSS! MY TEDDY'S EARS ARE ALL WET AND SOGGY! WHAT HAPPENED TO HIM?"

"OH NO! MY TEDDY'S EARS ARE SOPPY, TOO! "

"Heh. Heh. Sorry about that, girls."

We hiked on the gentle Hinman Fisherman Trail for about an hour, stopping often to give the girls a chance to look at things and explore the creek.

Aspen Leaves

We had to cross the cold creek a couple of times, and naturally, most of the little girls got their feet wet and screeched! Sammy got his feet wet and whined about it! I got my leathery-soled feet wet too, but it felt great! Some things never change.

The campsite was in a grove of aspen trees. There were plenty of baby aspen trees sprouting up, and I hoped that we'd be tethered close enough to them for us to have a little midnight *snackaroo* on the tender leaves. *Yum, yum!* But our people are usually very careful to prevent that, especially the mom who, as I told you before, just loves aspen trees. We do too, but for different reasons!

That night, when the green-hat girls roasted "hot dogs" on sticks, I looked around and was greatly relieved to see my Annie Dog still there, safe and sound and very much alive and well and not on the end of some stick! Next thing you know, those girls will probably want to roast "hot llamas" on a stick! *YIKES!*

After dinner, the troop gathered around the fire and howled along to the mom's guitar thing. They howled pretty loudly, but I noticed the sound of another sort of howling coming from up

140

the hill behind the campsite. These weren't people howls but the howls of a whole pack of coyotes! They had heard the girl pack howling, and I imagine that they were just inspired to join in. *"Yip, yip, awehoo! Yip, yip, awehoo!"*

The notes rose and fell in song, pretty music to my big banana ears, and the combination of people and animal howls sounded very melodic to me. But when the girls stopped before the animals did, one little girl heard them and screamed out,

"W O L V E S!!!"

This started the whole girl herd screaming. *YIKES!* My poor ears! Even Annie Dog tried to cover up her pointy German Shepherd ears, but it didn't help. Sometimes having big ears is a real curse!

Eventually the mom, who was the leader of the pack, calmed everyone down by telling them, "It's O.K. girls. They aren't wolves, just harmless coyotes! They won't hurt people. They're much more afraid of us than we are of them. And besides, we've got Annie and the llamas to protect us from any wild beasts."

After we heard her compliment, we made some brave guard dog and guard llama noises to impress and reassure the girls. They quieted down, thank goodness! But then, to take their minds off of the wild animal pack nearby, the mom told the girls that they could make s'mores, and they all started "Eeee-Yaah!" ....screeching again.

"OH NO!" moaned Annie. "OH NO!" moaned I. "OH, GREAT, S'MORES!" cried Sammy.

By the time the little girls all finished burning and eating these s'mores, they had

messy, sticky, chocolatey, marshmallowy, graham-crackery faces and hands. Yuck! Of course, they all had to come over and pat our heads goodnight, after which Annie then told me, "Your head now smells like a banana split, Dudley--two scoops of s'mores plopped between two big banana ears!" Then she laughed pretty hard at her own silly joke, and I just groaned at her.

Everyone *finally* got into their sleeping bags inside the tents and fell asleep, but the peace and quiet didn't last for long. The coyotes were pretty quiet, although they'd sneak up and spy on the girls from time to time. I'd give a soft warning whine and Annie would warn them with a quiet low growl, but mostly they were just being curious.

After about two hours of sleeping, the little girls started to get up to go to the bathroom, which they call "a camping latrine." Back and forth, back and forth, t*ramp, tramp, tramp* they went, shining their flashlights all over kingdom come, up in the trees and on the ground and i*n my eyes!* They whispered loudly and giggled out loud the whole time, and I wished that someone would give these girls tiptoe and whisper lessons, sooner than later!

I was *so* tired the next day from my night of disturbed sleep that the one hour pack trip out seemed to take forever. Sammy didn't complain but, instead, he remarked, "Aren't those little girls *fun*, Dudley? I can't wait for us to go out with them again! And that s'mores I found on the ground was so delicious! Hope I find s'more! Heh, heh."

He just amazes me, that Sammy, just amazes me!

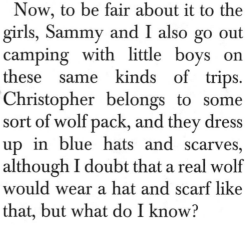

Now, to be fair about it to the girls, Sammy and I also go out camping with little boys on these same kinds of trips. Christopher belongs to some sort of wolf pack, and they dress up in blue hats and scarves, although I doubt that a real wolf would wear a hat and scarf like that, but what do I know?

Anyway, these wolf pack boys always make their campfires about four times too wide and three sizes too high and just about burn the woods down! Their camp is always *very* messy, and they burn most of their food and still think it tastes just great! Then, when their camping fiasco is all over, they make Sammy and me carry dirty, smoke-blackened pots and pans back home in our panniers. What a smelly, stinky, sooty mess! Our panniers smell like campfire smoke for weeks afterward!

The little blue boys also have a latrine area like the little green-hat girls do where they're supposed to go to the bathroom, but they never use it in the middle of the night. Mostly, they just step outside their tent and pee right there on the ground or on some poor tree next to their tent! Can you believe that?

Annie Dog says, "Little boys can be so uncouth!" So I think "uncouth" must be the German word for "yucky."

It so happens that llamas like to have latrine areas, too, and we try to use the same communal droppings area over and over, if we can. Our droppings are pretty much odorless and make good fertilizer, so llamas are pretty easy to clean up after. But when we're on a trail or stuck on our tether ropes, we just have to go where we happen to be stuck at the time.

People have to be careful with us when we cross cold streams because the cold water often sets off our bathroom clocks, and we'll start to go in the water--kind of like flush toilets. But we aren't *supposed* to pollute the streams like that, so the people try to hurry us through water crossings *before* those clocks go off. Sometimes I want to stop for a cold drink when I'm in the water, but they usually don't let me.

Also, you have to be very patient when a line of llamas decides to go to the bathroom because it can take us up to five minutes each. We don't have to go often, but *when we gotta' go, we REALLY gotta' go!,* if you know what I mean. And if *one* of us goes, that usually sets the rest of us off, too. So our bathroom breaks on the trail are

145

generally pretty long. Sorry about that!

But enough of this bathroom talk. How'd I get on that topic, anyway? Oh yes, now I remember--the little blue boys going outside of their tents at night. The more I think about that, I've decided that the wolf pack leaders must keep the little boys on tether ropes, just like us llamas, and that's why they don't go to the latrine area. Their tethers won't reach!

EPILOGUE

W ell, I could go on and on, but my writer friend tells me I need to end my book now. I haven't run out of stories, but my book has run out of pages!

Thank you for reading about my life. I enjoyed sharing it with you, and I hope my book has turned you into a "certified llama expert," since that was my main reason for writing it.

I worry that maybe I've done too much complaining about my family, but you know, I sometimes think that we get the most annoyed by the very ones we love the best. I'll bet it's like that in your family from time to time, too.

EPILOGUE

Living together isn't always the easiest thing in the world to do, and so sometimes we don't really appreciate one another until harm threatens. Then we circle the wagons around and protect each another, even with our very lives. Annie Dog says that's what *real* love is, *helping and taking good care of each other.* She even thinks that's why we're on this earth in the first place, to learn how to do that.

Now, I'm not certain if Annie Dog's right or not, but she *is* the wisest living creature I know, so I would tend to believe her.

From time to time, Sammy gets on my nerves, I've got to admit. But when all is said and done, I love him very much. I would be very lonely without my brother, that's for sure!

You already know what I think about my best friend, Annie Dog. And to be honestly perfect with you, even the cats aren't really that bad when you come right down to it. They certainly keep us amused, and they do *look* cute!

And the people in my family aren't really as awful as I might from time to time make them sound. I guess Sammy is right. I *do* exaggerate things a little bit, from time to time.

Annie Dog explains a lot about you humans to me, and it helps me to understand you better. You can't help it when you act human because that's exactly what you are. I've even learned to like your human hugs, although *not* your kisses yet!

148

EPILOGUE

All in all, I guess I'm a llucky llama. I'm very happy to be living with my family in the beautiful Colorado mountains, and I can't think of any llama I'd be willing to trade places with.

In the years to come, I hope to write about more adventures that Sammy and I are having and I hope you'll want to read about them, too. But for now, as the mom likes to say to the children, "See you later, alligator. After 'while, crocodile!"

You Gotta Llove a Llama

Diane White-Crane
arr. John R. Winkler

Hum hum hum hum (etc.)

hummm...   Hum hum   (etc.)

hum...   Oh you

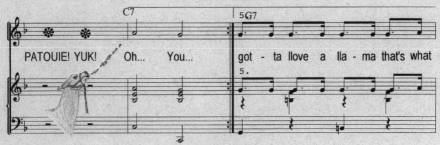

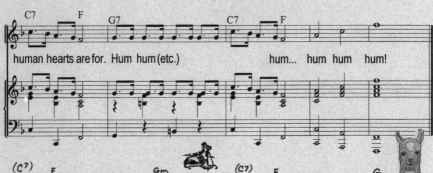

PATOUIE! YUK!   Oh...   You...   got - ta llove a lla - ma that's what

human hearts are for. Hum hum (etc.)   hum... hum hum hum!

2. Oh, you gotta llove a llama 'cause a llama has two toes,
With a soft pad on the bottom, feet just like the bucks and does.
They walk gently, they are quiet and you hardly know they're there,
But with a shrill whine they will warn you and help scare away a bear! WHOA! ROAR!!!

3. Oh, You gotta' llove a llama 'cause a llama likes to hum,
They will hum and hum and walk and hum until your hike is done.
They hum softly when they're happy they hum louder when they're mad.
And they'll hum to let you know when brother llama's being bad... HUM, HUM, HUM!

4. Oh, you gotta llove a llama 'cause a llama can be fun.
Once he knows for sure that you're the boss, you'll get your bidding done.
He will sometimes blow upon your neck with breath as sweet as hay,
Or he might rest his head upon your head and nuzzle you each day. AAWW! How Loving!!

5. Oh, you gotta' llove a llama 'cause a llama's smart and sweet,
And as far as pets that you could own, a llama can't be beat!
Oh, you gotta' llove a llama and I won't say anymore....
'cept you gotta' llove a llama, that's what human hearts are for. Hum, hum, hum, ...,..., ...,
Humm, Humm, Humm, Hummmm!

Also by author:

Best Seller
HIKING the 'BOAT
A Guidebook to 30 Trails in the Steamboat Springs Area,
with Special Notes on How and Where to Hike with Children.

Aspentree Press, P.O. Box 775051
Steamboat Springs, Colorado 80477-5051
ISBN 0-9631322-0-2